War Bride

AVA SINCLAIR

Pandora's Box
Publishing

One

PROLOGUE

I am darkness. I am rage.

They say I have no name, but I do. Only my kind know it.

Soon, my enemies will know it too, and will speak it with quavering voices as they kneel before me to beg for mercy I will not show.

I am Seadus, King of the ShadowFell, and I will have my victory. I will have my vengeance.

In the time before time, it was the ShadowFell who gave others of our kind their first taste of fear. Dragons think themselves invincible until faced with the only thing that can best them—a stronger dragon. There used to be other dragon clans on this side of the world. One by one, we drove them all away.

Only man and beast remained. For the ShadowFell, mankind served a minor purpose. Just as Night Bears do not kill the bees that produce the honey they crave, neither did we kill the humans who produced the cattle and sheep we occasionally took.

1

The humans would try to defend their flocks, shooting clumsy spears in our direction, but their weapons were no more effective against dragons than bee stings against bears.

Then a new race arose, created by the God and Goddess of the Wyld. Drakoryans. Half man, half dragon. It was those meddlesome hybrids that saw a broader use for the humans. In need of both meat to feed their dragon side and grain to feed their human side, they brought the humans under their protection and rule.

This was not to be borne. Only we were allowed to rule, and thus began the first war between the ShadowFell and the Drakoryan.

I, Seadus, who had never known defeat, felt it first from the Drakoryan and found it bitter.

There have been three wars with the Drakoryan. Each has ended with our defeat. Our enemy battles not with dragon strength alone, but with the tactics of man.

A dragon can hem another dragon into a crevasse. But a dragon that shifts into a human can land and disappear into the mountains. A dragon commands other dragons alone, but a dragon who turns into a man can command an army of men with weaponry designed by those who know a dragon's vulnerability.

After our first defeat, the God of Deep Places sent his emissary with an offer of aid so offensive that I drove him away with fire.

I am proud. My kind is proud.

But he came again after the last defeat, taunting us in our sleep. Without help from the God of Deep Places, the next defeat would be our last. There was a path to victory for the Shadow-Fell, he whispered, not just of the Drakoryan Empire, but of the whole of the magical realm above. The God of the Deep Places promised us more than glory. He promised us dominance and limitless power.

Did we not realize, he asked, that the Drakoryan rely on humans for more than just cattle and grain? They used human females to perpetuate their numbers. Then he repeated the offer I'd found so offensive.

Victory for the ShadowFell would mean becoming man-dragons ourselves. The she-dragon — the mother of us all who produces without a mate— would no longer produce the great dragons of old. Dark magic would change her offspring into smaller, quicker dragons. Dragon soldiers that we would command come time of war.

As we awoke, we would begin raiding the villages ruled by the Drakoryans. We would take the maidens.

And when all the soldiers were hatched from the Mother Eggs, the God of Deep Places said we would take the Mystic Mountain and plunder its magic to transform into those like the Drakoryan, but with an army of mindless dragon soldiers to serve us. We would kill the Drakoryans, and put the humans under our rule to grow our food and serve in our armies. We would be dragon lords, commanding armies of dragons and men. We would be invincible.

Ultimate power. Ultimate rule. Ultimate vengeance.

After ages of defeat, the promise of victory was too tempting to ignore.

When we began to wake again, one by one, the whispered promise of the God of Deep Places was fresh in our minds. We began the first of our raids on the outer villages, refining our plans.

We'd planned to attack the rest of the villages at once, ready to fight the defending Drakoryans if we had to. But on the night of the final raid, we found the villages empty. The Drakoryans did not stand in defense of the villages. They had evacuated them to the stronghold of the Drakoryan Empire.

Our fury was great. We burned all the village cottages in our rage. We roared our displeasure at the God of Deep Places.

But he only laughed. The Drakoryans had played into our hands, he said. We would use fire to turn the villagers they protected against them.

Two

ISLA

When I was a little girl, a man of our village lost his lower leg to a Night Bear. His misfortune became a macabre fascination for me and my friends. We would gather around, querying him about the attack, cringing as he described the bear's teeth tearing through flesh and bone. The bear was as big as a tree, he said, perhaps bigger. His account both terrified and enthralled us, but even more interesting than the bear's savagery was the injury itself.

"Does it hurt?" we'd ask, marveling at the scars that remained where the village healer had sewn the skin together over the bony stump. Some adults would have boxed our ears for such rudeness, but the crippled man was kind, and bore our questions with humor.

Of course, it had hurt, he said, and while it no longer did, he'd discovered there was something worse than physical pain. Sometimes, he told us, he would wake and forget he did not have a leg. He fancied he could still feel it. His knee would ache, even though there was no knee. His foot would itch, even though there was no foot. The sensations were so convincing that he would rise from bed only to fall to the floor, his stump throbbing with hurt.

As a child, I found this all very fanciful. How could a man forget he had no foot? How could he feel something that was not there?

Only after my village was destroyed by the ShadowFell did I finally understand. Some mornings as I stir awake I move to the left side of the bed, expecting to feel the warm body of my sister Zara, or imagining that I smell the morning porridge Mother is cooking, or that I hear my father's cart rolling away as he heads to the fields. I smile, ready for another day as steady and dependable as a leg.

Then, like the man in my village, I remember. And the loss comes crashing back, the absence pulsing through me like an ache.

I was the only one left alive in the village of Branlock after the black dragons stole away my fellow maidens and slaughtered everyone else. The Drakoryans who found the carnage saved my life. They say I belong to them now, that they will become my new kith and kin. The Lords of Za'vol — Jayx, Turin, and Zyvis—are big men, light of hair and bronze of skin. When I sit surrounded by them, I feel as small as a child, and as helpless. They exude raw power that would make me feel protected were I not so afraid of them, of what they want.

They want me.

"Isla of Branlock," they've said each morning since I arrived at Castle Za'vol. "How does this day find you?"

Each time, I try to force a smile, but it is still so hard. Even when solicitous, the smoldering in their eyes reminds me that these three huge dragon lords took me for a reason. They will have their due, grief or no, for they burn with a lust that cannot be contained.

After the Drakoryans had pulled me unconscious from the well where I'd hidden, they'd returned with me to Castle Fra'hir, where they'd been holding council. It was there I'd met Lyla, Lady of Fra'hir, who'd once been a villager like me. From her, I learned the truth about my rescuers.

She said there are bad dragons in this world, like the ShadowFell, but that there are good dragons, too, and that it was the good dragons who had borne me to safety. She said those good dragons were Drakoryans – a race that could transform into men. It was the Drakoryans who claimed village maidens from the Altar Rocks. For centuries, we'd assumed our sisters, daughters, and friends had perished. But they had not died. They'd lived and been mated to dragon men.

Now, she told me, the Drakoryans are going to war with the ShadowFell that slaughtered my people. The villagers have been brought into the Drakoryan valley for protection. Many things would change, including the Drakoryan tradition of claiming virgin sacrifices from villages. With conflict looming, some lords would be allowed special permission to take war brides.

I would be mated to my rescuers – the Lords of Za'vol. This was, she assured me, an honor. But I did not feel honored. I did not want to hear this. I wanted nothing to do with any dragon.

The Lady of Fra'hir had remained quiet as I'd swept all the pretty bottles and vials from her dressing table in a helpless rage. Only when I calmed myself did she approach me. She did not condescend, but neither did she indulge my pity.

"You cannot change the past," she'd said. "But you can shape your future. You cannot bring your village back, but you can forge a legacy that honors those who built it." She'd taken my hands and looked in my eyes. Her gaze was braver than any man's. "You will go with the Lords of Za'vol. You will learn that just as not all men are noble, not all dragons are monsters." She'd smiled then. "And you will find your strength. The girl who clung to life in the bottom of a well survived for a reason. She has a purpose. Go with them. Go and find it."

This morning it is the eldest, Lord Jayx, who comes to greet me.

"Isla of Branlock? How did you sleep?"

He is sturdy and broad-shouldered with sun-kissed skin and a silver scar that traverses the muscle mounds of his chest. He has hair the color of summer wheat and eyes the color of ice.

He seeks to be gentle, but underneath I sense a fraying rope of tension holding something back, something wild and dangerous. When he asks me if I'd like to walk with him, he does not even try to hide the erection that tents his leather skirt. None of them do, these lords.

Today he tells me the history of Castle Za'vol. Drakoryans are not named for their fathers or mothers, but for the mountains they claim when they reach adulthood. There are many castles on the ranges around the Drakoryan Empire, all ancient, all carved by witch magic. Castle Za'vol is a steep, cloud-shrouded peak that overlooks a plain to the south dotted by growing villages of refugees saved before the ShadowFell could attack any more villages.

Mount Za'vol overlooks smaller peaks to the north. A higher one looms to the west. There is a flanking wall on this side of the castle. This is where Lord Jayx takes me today.

I have not been to this part of the castle. The wall reaches a dizzying height. Moist clouds surround us. Lord Jayx says it is not always like this, but on this day, the clouds make it difficult for me to see him. He looks like a shadow in the mist, even though he stands beside me.

"You are in mourning," he says.

I don't reply. Instead I strain my eyes to find a shape in the fog, a peak, a raven, anything.

"I will not pretend that you have not suffered great hurt, Isla of Branlock. I will not pretend that you will ever fully heal from your loss. But neither will I pretend that we can go on like this. Lady Lyla told you what would be expected of you here."

"I know what is expected." I peer into the swirling mist. "You and your mighty brothers will take me to your bed chambers and fuck me. I will endure it, because that is what I have been taught to do as a villager, isn't it? To endure the rule of the great Drakoryans, or suffer the consequences?"

There's a sigh in the fog. "What we did..."

"...was your right as rulers. I know."

I look over at him. "Lord Jayx, I will not pretend to want any of this if you will not pretend that your patience is kindness. In the end, you will get what you want. Dragons always get what they want, whether it is the daughters of villagers or the destruction of a village itself." I pause. "Regardless of what the Lady of Fra'hir says, you are all the same."

I can now make out enough of his features to see a spasm of hurt cross his face.

"No." His tone is still kind, but there's steel in it now. "We are *not* all the same." He pauses. "But you are right. We do get what we want." He looks away. "Tomorrow, my brothers and I will battle in dragon form for first rights to your body. In the past, this battle decided which brother claimed a virgin from Altar Rock. No villager has ever witnessed this combat. We want you to see your lords fight with flame and tooth and claw, so that you may know what we risk for the privilege of taking one so precious. We consider lying with you to be an honor, Isla of Branlock, an honor so great as to temporarily turn brother against brother."

The mist is starting to clear farther out. I can see the

mountain peaks, the craggy depths of the ravine below. I try to imagine dragon fighting dragon over *me*, a woman pulled half dead from the depths of a well.

I can feel Jayx staring at me. His gaze caresses me like hands. He is close enough that I can feel the heat from his body warming me through the mist.

"And after that?" I ask, although I know what will happen. I shudder. It is easier to imagine these men warring as dragons than to imagine them taking me with anything other than roughness.

Jayx doesn't immediately answer.

"Afterwards, the victor will take his ease in the healing pools of our castle long enough to mend his wounds and regain his strength. Then he will come to you, Isla of Branlock. He will lay you on the bed and fight a new battle, one that has him control his lust, which is stronger than any dragon. And he will, for it will be his duty to introduce you to the carnal mysteries, to show you how a masterful lord can play the strings of your body's instrument to perfect pitch, to use his fingers and tongue and cock to draw you away — even for a moment — from the awful pain of your loss. You will drift on an ocean of sensation. You will rise and fall on waves of pleasure. And the only cry you utter will be for your lover to end the misery of your virginity and to fill you with his cock."

His words have the strangest effect on me. My legs feel heavy, as if rooting me to the mountain under my feet. I gasp and realize that I had been holding my breath. Yet, it is the soft, curious throb between my thighs that is most unnerving. It as if Lord Jayx has stirred something in me that had died the day the dragon destroyed my village.

I know what it is. *Desire*.

Oh, yes, I have felt it. In my village, we were discouraged, from experiencing such feelings. We were to stay as untouched maidens for three years after the age of claiming, to give the Drakoryans time to take or pass us by. If we weren't claimed in that time, we could mate with one of our own. There were village boys who would return from the fields, their sleek, ropy arms and lean torsos glistening with sweat. I would draw water for them, and when I handed them a cup they would fix me with slow, easy smiles and hungry eyes. I remember their faces. I remember the tingling pulses of budding need I felt in their presence.

Those boys are dead now. Only I have survived, along with a need that feels like a betrayal of their memory. It is a need as primal as the dragon lords who plucked me from the well where I used to draw water for hopeful village lads.

Three

TURIN

Change is in the air. Change in the empire. Change in Castle Za'vol. Change in me and my brothers.

Sometimes I think all women are witches, and the most powerful are the ones working unintentional magic. Isla of Branlock was half drowned and close to death when I found her, but the mere flutter of her eyelids, the glimpse of her green eyes, cast a spell on me more powerful than anything conjured in the Mystic Mountain.

I barely slept last night, and when I roll from my side to my back this morning, I look down to see the sheet peaked across my aching loins. I wonder if my brothers woke with the same desperate need, but when I think of them, another feeling sweeps over me: hatred.

I do not like this, although my father, Lord Egir of Im'Ril, warned me these feelings of animosity are normal and will pass after the battle.

When Father came to the castle yesterday, we shifted

together and sparred for practice. Afterwards, he said it brought back memories of how he and his brothers fought for my mother, Lady Klea.

He told me the battle between sons often stirs the fire of the long-settled rivalry of their fathers. Every Drakoryan wants first rights. Every Drakoryan father wants the same for his son.

I am faster and stronger than my father now, and even as he lamented his age, he was proud when I bested him. Still, he cautioned that it would not be so easy on the morrow. He'd reminded me that my brothers will be equally fierce, that the lust building within us will become white-hot rage as we take to the skies. Fraternal battles draw a Drakoryan dangerously close to a fully primal dragon state. Only defeat or victory can snap us out of it.

While my father spoke almost wistfully of this contest, part of me resents having to fight for Isla of Branlock. I was the one who found her. I was the one who saved her, who bore her back to Castle Fra'hir, where all the Drakoryan had gathered for Council. I was the one who'd lowered her into the healing pool.

I was the one who'd saved her life, but that does not matter. Today, I will enjoy no favor as I fight for her because this battle is a necessary tradition.

Dragons are contentious by nature, even with one another. Sharing a mate forces a house to build cooperation as one would build a muscle. The results are the same: strength.

The battle for first rights forges the path towards that cooperation. We are taught to seek a balance in combat – to balance our dragon lust for victory with the humanity that keeps us from taking the battle too far.

As eager as I am to fight, I am equally eager for it to be over.

I rise from my bed and go to the wash basin. I dip my hands in the water, watching as steam curls around them. My blood runs hot in my veins. I can barely stand still. I splash my face and the droplets instantly evaporate from my fevered skin. I am famished. I need to eat.

There is already a feast laid out when I arrive in the hall, thanks to my mother who is visiting Castle Za'vol with my fathers. My younger brother, Zyvis, glares at me from over a whole suckling pig. Beside him, Jayx, the eldest, is starting on his second peafowl, the first reduced to a heap of bones. Even though there is no blaze in the great stone fireplace, sweat beads on their brows.

We are all heat and appetite, and on this morning communicate only through glares and glowers. I take a seat and begin reaching for food. When I grab for a beef joint, Jayx tries to snatch it away even though his plate is full. Our eyes meet and his flame with competitive rage. I pull the meat away from him and grab a second piece with my other hand, wordlessly daring him to try and take it.

"My boys have such appetites this morning." Our mother enters the room. She is aging slowly and gracefully, retaining the beauty that Jayx's father first saw when he snatched her from the Altar Rock of her village. He bested his brothers. Will I best mine today? I want to, more than anything.

"Good morning, Mother," I say, grateful for the diversion. Even the inner dragons so desperate to emerge and fight are no match for maternal authority. Her presence has a calming effect. Zyvis and Jayx greet her as well.

"I have missed feeding you," she says, settling at the head of the table. Her mouth quirks into a smile. "I'd also forgotten how much you eat. The appetites of your fathers have slowed, but don't tell them I said so."

"Where are they?" Jayx asks.

"Already on the wall." She smirks. "Already arguing over who will win."

"Why do they argue over something with so obvious an

answer?" Zyvis tosses aside a freshly cleaned bone. "Of course I'll win. By this time tomorrow, I'll have both stoked and quenched the fire burning between the legs of our flame-haired beauty." He smiles confidently.

"You?" Jayx scoffs. "You've allowed your father to fill your head with false hope. Isla requires a practiced hand to guide her to the paths of pleasure, and I have more skill than all of you combined."

I know I shouldn't take the bait, but I can't help it. "Jayx, just because you have sheathed your lance in the slick scabbard of every household maid in the empire doesn't mean you are skilled in the art of loving, only the art of rutting." I fix both my brothers with a hard stare. "I'll see you both dashed on the rocks before you touch Isla."

"You'll see nothing!" Jayx is on his feet. His eyes burn gold. I stand too and lift a goblet, flinging it to the side. Fury pounds in my ears and I am aware of Zyvis' chair falling over backwards as he rises as well.

"SIT!" Our mother's voice is like a dash of cold water thrown in our faces. "*Sit*," she hisses again. Her arms are crossed. We obey.

Mother frowns at us until we turn our attention to her. "I did not come all this way to see you fight before your time. I came to advise you, in the hopes that what I have to say will be remembered after this battle." She looks from one of us to the other. "There will only be one victor today. One. There will be two losers."

She glares at us until she's sure we're listening. "One of you will take Isla to your bedchamber tonight. The other two will seek your lonely beds. You will all eventually have your time with this woman, but as one who was once in Isla's place, heed my advice. It is not your body, nor even your heart that should lead this dance. Follow your heads, my sons, not your cocks. There is more sex between a woman's ears than between her legs.

"Your little virgin survived for days in a well," our mother continues. "She is strong willed, and strong minded. Embrace the all of her; as you seek to teach, make yourself a pupil of her passion. Do this, and she will embrace you in return. Do this, and forge the way for the Deepening, and with it the kind of bond you will all need to carry you through these dark times."

Her words are sobering. Our focus on Isla has nearly made us forget why we're being allowed to take her now. War is coming. The ShadowFell who burned the villages of Kenrick and Branlock have stirred awake. By now they must know the villagers have been relocated to the Drakoryan Empire. How long before they bring the fight here?

"Our fathers expect the War Council to be called any day," I remark grimly, drawing glances from my brothers. "Should the council be assembled, King Vukurcis will expect all lords to travel to his castle. He will not allow delays, not even for a mating. We may not all have time to claim our maiden."

My brothers and I turn our energy back to our food, feeding ravenously, the line between human and dragon as thin as a membrane, the tension as thick as the brown bread we eat with our meat.

The meal is exhausted all too quickly. So is the time for waiting. My mother rises. We stand in deference and watch her leave. She is going to fetch Isla, to take her to the flanking wall where she will join our parents to watch us battle for first rites.

With Mother gone, my brothers and I remain alone at the table. The room is filled with the sound of breathing which grows more ragged by the second. I feel hot sweat pouring down my face. My heart bursts with the desire to fly and fight. My brothers feel it too. We rise and leave out different doors. When we next confront one another, it will be as dragons.

Four

ISLA

I'm standing in a line of strangers, cloudy sky above, a craggy gorge below. To my left is Lady Klea, as distant and regal as a queen. She wears the same stoic expression as her trio of mates, the Lords of Im'Ril. They stand to my right, and in them I see a resemblance to the men who will soon take to the skies as dragons and battle for the right to claim me.

I pull the fur collar of the cape up against my neck. The cape and the high-necked green gown it covers were both gifts from Lady Klea, who came by my room to greet me this morning. I'd just finished my solitary breakfast of salted beef and stewed pears when she arrived.

I'd braced myself upon meeting her, expecting her to condescend, to tell me how fortunate I was that her sons had chosen me. But she delivered both her gift and the accompanying compliment with an aloofness that I suspect is born of natural reserve.

"You'll need to become accustomed to having nice things.

It is an adjustment of its own kind, the Drakoryan generosity." She'd nodded towards a maid who approached to hold out the finest garments I'd ever seen. "You'll wear these today, although I'm not sure anything could do your beauty justice."

She'd turned then and departed without another word. The maid was about my age, a sturdy girl who introduced herself as Sal before flashing me a nervous, gap-toothed smile.

"I'm to fix your hair. And dress you." She issued these statements as if they were settled matters, so I assumed she was acting on Lady Klea's orders. Until that moment, I'd refused all offers of a personal maid. I'd considered sending her away, but when I saw the lacing on the gown, I realized I could not fasten it alone, so I'd allowed Sal to direct me to the dressing table.

I'd ignored her curious glances in the looking glass as she'd brushed and plaited my hair in a thick braid down my back. Sal had been efficient and detached as she'd replaced my shift with Lady Klea's gift. Made of heavy velvet lined with satin, the gown seemed more fit for a princess than for a simple girl from Branlock. The cloak was so sumptuous that were there any room for joy in my aching heart, I'd surely have felt it. But I'd only felt numb as I stared into the looking glass.

"You're so lucky." Sal had uttered the words as she closed the jeweled clasp at the top of the cloak.

"Lucky?" I was barely able to get the word out, so great was my shock. "My village was burned, and my family killed save for my sister, who was taken."

My maid had just shrugged as she'd turned to pick up my nightdress from the floor. "Still lucky," she'd muttered. "You'll be a lady now."

I consider her words now as I look out over the wall. What does this place do to human women?

At my side, Lady Klea stands in thoughtful silence. She'd once been stolen away by a dragon, but accepted her fate,

18

abandoning all that she knew. Sal, who belongs to a serving class not claimed as Drakoryan mates, sees my circumstance as good fortune. Even Lady Lyla urged me to adapt.

As I look down and see the Lords of Za'vol each emerge from the mouths of three different caves, I know it will be more of a challenge than anyone realizes. The hair on the back of my neck rises and feel a chill run through my body despite the richness of my fur cloak.

I know what these men are about to become.

Five

ZYVIS

I expect you to win.

The words of my father still ring in my ears, intensifying the pressure I feel as I walk out onto the ledge.

Yesterday, I'd been on one of the western battlements watching Turin spar with his father when my own had approached. I'd immediately felt the tension draw and tighten the cords of my muscles.

My father, Lord Udra, had once been a regimental commander. I've spent my entire life trying and failing to live up to his expectations.

Drakoryans age far slower than humans, but like great mountains, even dragon lords wear over time. There is more gray than blonde in my father's beard now, and while he is still strong, he has slowed more than his younger brothers, and walks with a slight limp he tries to hide. When war comes, it will grieve him not to take to the battlefield. He lives through me now, and I do not allow myself to resent it. He is my father, and must be respected.

He'd been silent as we stood on the windswept battlement watching Turin and Lord Egir practice.

"You're faster than Turin," he'd finally said. "You'll easily beat him." He'd waved dismissively towards the scene below, as if his words made this settled fact. "Now, Jayx—he'll be your competition." My father had puffed out the broad barrel of his chest. "But even Jayx will be no match for *my* son. He lacks the cunning and strength you inherited. Preparation still matters, however." He'd turned to me then, his voice gruff. "Have you watched Jayx spar?"

"Of course," I'd said.

"And what did you learn?" He barked the question like the commander he used to be, so I'd answered as the son he expected.

"He favors the left, Father, so I should watch my left flank. Jayx also rolls to escape an attack, so I should hem him in when I can.

"Drive him towards the ground if you have to." My father's tone was hard.

That advice had given me pause. "If I do that, and he's still rolling..." I'd looked down at the jagged rocks, imagining how this strategy could end. "If he doesn't pull up..."

"You want to win, don't you?" I could feel his glare, as cold and sharp as the wind. "Or would you bring shame to my legacy? He'll pull up, Zyvis. He's too smart to bash himself on the rocks, but too proud to pull up soon enough to keep his bearings. He'll be disoriented from the roll. Use your fire to force a landing. That's how you'll prevail."

Jayx's father, Lord Orys, had bested mine in the battle for our mother and now the mighty Lord Udra would have vengeance through his son. He'd had me repeat the strategy back to him, word for word, until he was satisfied that the moves I made were his moves, that my victory would be his.

As I stand on the ledge, I still feel a sting of shame over my moment of worry for Jayx. My father is right. With so much at stake, now is not the time for weakness. Now is the time for glory.

For myself.

For my father.

I can see all of them standing on the wall. My father, the largest, looks confident. Lord Egir and Lord Orys stand at his side. My mother is at the end. Between them is Isla, the prize I must win.

When my brothers emerge onto nearby ledges, I allow my hatred for them to rise in my blood like poison. Despite the icy winds, I am burning inside. I throw my head back and let the fire overtake me.

It is time.

My blood is a river of heat. I can feel it coursing through me, burning my human form from inside out. As the flame consumes me, I know I should cling to my humanity, to balance my rage with rational thought, with mercy. But my father's face invades my mind and something slips. The human voice in my head is a whisper as I am obliterated by a violet flame. Rage fills my chest as I solidify into my dragon form. I inhale, catching the sweet scent my prize on the wind. I stretch out my neck and whip my head around, golden eyes seeking my brothers.

And there they are. Jayx is now an indigo dragon; Turin one of sunset orange. I open my mouth and emit a roar that shakes the valley. Ravens lift from the crags below and take flight, winging their way from the impending danger.

I drop from the ledge and spread my wings, banking west and heading towards the wall where the woman I plan to win stands with our mother and our fathers. I will woo her with my might. I will show her that I am the strongest. I will show them all. Isla is ashen-faced as I fly towards the wall. I veer at the last minute, a violaceous streak across the sky. From my peripheral vision, I catch a glimpse of deep blue. Just as my father warned, Jayx is approaching from the left. Hatred for him and Turin, who is above and to my right, thrums through my body.

I pump my wings, shooting high through the clouds. I inhale gulps of air as I rise. It slows my ascent, but there is a strategy to what I do. With my massive lungs filled, I am ready to release the fire venom into my throat. I arc, diving back toward the ground. As I break back through the clouds, I see Turin heading towards Jayx. It infuriates me. I have planned to expend the bulk of my strength on Jayx—our eldest brother, and my strongest opponent.

I change tactics, banking to the right and releasing enough venom to ignite a flame I direct at the annoying Turin. I am rewarded with a scream as fire catches him on a wing joint. It is not a direct hit, but enough to make him veer away.

I head for Jayx, imagining Isla marveling at my speed. I think of my father's pride. I think of how I hate my brothers. I bear down on Jayx, giving him no time to move above me. I drive him towards a crevasse. As predicted, he starts to roll. I have seen him do this before. He seeks to roll into an upward spin, gaining an advantage once he's above me. Yet when I'm almost upon him, I spread my wings, cutting off the room he needs to ascend back through the narrowing passage.

Jayx begins to spiral. Somewhere in my mind, I hear a human voice – my own – telling me to pull up, to give him room to rise. But the louder voice of my father screams for me to wait, lest Jayx recover with an advantage. I am lost in my rage. I continue to follow the spinning form of the indigo dragon downward as the jagged rocks rise to meet him.

I'm so focused on Jayx that the glancing blow from the

side takes me by surprise. I feel all the air I'd reserved for flame forced from my lungs as I slam into the side of the crevasse. I slide down the slope, snapping off trees and dislodging boulders before rolling from one ledge and slamming into another below. The world spins around me.

As I struggle to reorient myself I realize what has happened.

Turin. As I'd focused on Jayx, our middle brother had flown down and under my spread wing to sideswipe me, allowing Jayx to recover from his spin moments before he would have hit the ground. I see a blue flash as our eldest shoots past where I lie, back up through the crevasse.

I suck in enough air to roar in indignation as I clamber to my feet.

To regain enough speed to rejoin the fight, I need room to dive and rise, but the ledge I've landed on is not high enough for that. I can only take off by ascending, and before I can, Jayx is above me. He's diving into the crevasse, his gold eyes narrowed in determination. I see the white daggers of his teeth, the open cavern of his mouth, and the fireball forming at the back of his throat a split second before a wave of intense heat hits me, searing my scales and fracturing the thin rock beneath me. I am falling again, and this time when I hit the ground there is no recovering. I am too burned, too broken, too bruised.

I have lost.

The battle is between my brothers now. I look to the sky, watching as Jayx now pursues Turin. They rise above the clouds and the mountaintops shake with their roars. They drop through the clouds, their talons clutched together. Jayx has his teeth clenched on the base of Turin's orange neck by his shoulder.

But Turin – whom I sorely underestimated – is still able to crane his head above where his rival's teeth are latched. He aims a burst of fire over Jayx's back, burning the length of his right wing.

Jayx opens his mouth to scream, breaking his hold. The only thing holding Jayx aloft now is Turin's grip on his talons. Jayx's burnt wing flops limply at his side. If Turin were to release him, Jayx would fall to his death. But Turin keeps his grip, dipping low enough to drop our brother safely on a ledge.

A shaft of sun breaks through the clouds, illuminating Turin's orange scales as he circles menacingly over Jayx.

Jayx tries to pump his wings—a useless effort, but who can blame him? Turin responds by setting some trees nearby alight, a reminder that he has the advantage. Even if Jayx could make fire, Turin can avoid it from the air.

The dragon that is Jayx bellows in despair before erupting into an indigo flame that shrinks into his man form. Turin, roaring in victory, circles the valley before perching on the ledge where Isla waits with our fathers and mother.

The battle is over. Turin, who saved Isla from the well in Branlock, is the victor. I should feel happy for him, yet I only feel humiliation and rage at being the first to face defeat in the battle of brothers.

Six

ISLA

Growing up in Branlock accustomed me to the sound of dragon wings, the heat of fire in the night as they burnt what fields villagers aren't allowed to plant. A taken from Branlock, but I was just a child then. Only adults are allowed to witness a claiming, so my first real look at a dragon was when the ShadowFell slaughtered my village. I was unconscious when the Drakoryans had taken me from the ruins of Branlock and because they'd not wanted to frighten me, I'd been given a sleeping draught before the Lords of Za'vol had taken me home from Castle Fra'hir. Lyla had warned me that it might frighten me to see the Lords of Za'vol change for the first time. I don't think she realized that first time would be the day their battle.

What they'd intended as a proof of devotion, I saw as a display of savagery. The screams still ring in my ears and when Turin transforms, I cannot separate the man he becomes from the creature he was. I stand rooted to the spot as Lord Egir walks over to embrace his son, his bearded face radiating a father's pride.

"You fought well, Turin."

Even Lord Orys manages a smile. "I would have preferred it be Jayx, but we are all family." He looks at his other brother. "Right, Udra?"

Lord Udra does not offer his congratulations. "It is easy for you to say. Your son did not come in last." He turns away without another word, stalking towards the tunnels.

"Turin has won you." A soft voice gets my attention. It's Lady Klea, but I can barely comprehend her words through the pounding in my ears. Turin is looking past his father, at me. I can tell by his hopeful expression that he seeks my approval most of all, yet as he takes a step towards me, panic swells in my breast and I back away, shaking my head.

"No. No. No." I point directly at him. "Stay back!" I shout the words so loudly they echo back to me from the rocks around us. "Stay back! Stay back! Stay back!"

Turin stops in his tracks. His bare, muscular chest is heaving. Down below I can see his defeated brothers limping into the caves, heading towards the healing pools.

"Isla..." The voice that calls my name is not Turin's but his mother's. She steps between the two of us. Over her shoulder I see Turin's father cast a worried glance in his brother's direction. Lady Klea turns to them.

"My lords, it is a time for celebration. The battle is over. Lord Udra has no doubt gone to the pools to praise Zyvis for his hard-fought effort. Lord Egir, take Turin to heal as well. Lord Orys, you should go see to Jayx." She puts her arm around me. "I will escort Isla to her bedchamber."

There's steel in her soft words and I am grateful when the men turn and walk away. Turin glances back at me as he goes. In spite of the cold wind, there's a sheen of sweat on his back, bare and broad above the leather skirt he wears. The back of his arm from the middle of the bulging bicep to halfway down his forearm is covered in huge blisters, but I know the pain in his eyes has more to do with my reaction than his injury.

Lady Klea is as taciturn on our return to my bedchamber as she was on our walk to the wall. We enter to find Sal dozing in a chair by the fire, her head lolling to the side.

"Up!" Lady Klea's sharp command startles the maid from her sleep. "This room is chill, girl. Stoke the blaze and then fetch mulled wine and oat cakes for us. A lady's maid does not dally by the fire. Should I hear of your lazing again, it'll be kitchen work for you. Understand?"

As Sal's ruddy face reddens further, I wonder if issuing such commands will come naturally to me one day. I might defend the woman sent to serve me, if I weren't so overwhelmed by my own circumstance.

Lady Klea goes to stand by the window. Her back is to me, and she waits for Sal to leave before she turns to face me. Her quiet scrutiny unnerves me.

"You have no need to fear my sons," she finally says. "You will accept Turin when he comes to you."

"You have no right to judge my fear." Indignation has ignited my spirit. "And I am no serving girl for you to scold and command."

I brace myself for Lady Klea's anger, but instead, she laughs, softly at first, and then harder.

"Oh my," she says when she composes herself. "I do believe I like you, Isla of Branlock. Behind that frightened façade, I sense a fighter." She walks over to me and reaches out a cool hand to brush my face. "You will need that fight, I think, for there is no escape from this life."

"Lady Lyla told me as much, but what use is a fighting spirit in a world that requires me to capitulate to monsters?"

"You are young, Isla of Branlock, too young to realize the power in submission." She arches a brow. "Or, at least, in the illusion of submission. The strongest dragon lord – or dragon for that matter – is weaker than a cunning female. A Drako-ryan male's bloodline depends on his mate's willing acceptance of his advances. He cannot ravish her. He cannot abuse her. He must curry her favor if she is ever to grow his seed." She pauses. "The dragons who killed your family have no such investment in the women they took."

My eyes fill with tears at her words.

"They have my sister," I say, nearly choking on the words.

Lady's Klea's face softens. She nods. "I know. My sons told me." She takes my face in her hands. "Now you listen to me. If the ShadowFell had intended to kill your sister or the other women, they would have done it. She's still alive." Her eyes search mine. "You feel it, don't you?"

I nod wordlessly. "Yes." A tear trails down my face and she wipes it away with the pad of her thumb. "I want to kill the dragon that took her."

"I don't doubt that." She studies my face. "Isla, I can't replace your mother. I won't pretend to know what she'd say at a moment like this. You must have gotten your strength from someone, and strong mothers have strong daughters. Somewhere, your sister is being strong. You must be strong until you can see her again." She grows quiet. "Turin will be here soon. You are every bit as fierce as a dragon. Show him. Show them all. Use what weapons you have until you can gain the ones you want."

Seven

JAYX

I have never known such pain. The arm that was my wing was so badly burnt, I feared the pools might not completely heal it. That is not the only thing yet to heal. Anger still burns hot in my veins.

Were it not for Turin, Zyvis would have killed me. My father, who lowered me into the healing waters, is quiet. Zyvis nurses his wounds in another pool. His father does not kneel at his side. Lord Udra's broad back is turned to his son.

"Move your arm." My father reaches into the water to cup my elbow. I wince. While skin is mending, movement is still excruciating. I must force myself to flex the injured limb.

"I'm sorry, Father," I say. "I know you wanted me to win."

My father cups some water into his hand and dribbles it over my shoulder. He's missing half his thumb on his left hand, and I remember him telling me that Udra bit it off when they were sparring as adolescent dragons. A dragon can heal of burns and breaks, but a missing body part is beyond the springs' power to repair.

"You have nothing to apologize for, Jayx. You fought bravely. And you fought fairly."

He speaks the last line loud enough to carry through the cavern. Zyvis flinches and Lord Udra's grim expression proves that my father's barb hit more than one intended target.

"Just be grateful that your son did not shame you." Lord Udra takes a step towards my father, who rises. Both men are tense. For a moment, I think they are going to fight. Instead, my father's brother turns and walks from the cave.

Zyvis stares at the wall, and as much as I try to muster sympathy for him, I cannot. In my mind's eye, I can still see him barreling towards me as the ground below grew closer.

Our middle brother walks in now.

"Turin." My father approaches him and his father. "Well fought."

"Thank you." Turin nods, as Lord Egir claps my father on the back.

"What do you say we share a bumper of ale to celebrate the bond our sons will soon form with Isla?"

Turin's gaze moves to Zyvis, and I see my concern reflected in his eyes. Our youngest brother does not congratulate Turin, and Turin does not speak to him as he joins me in my pool. What should be a time of personal and physical healing between brothers is cast in a shadow of mistrust.

Discord among Drakoryan brothers is rare, but tension does exist. We sensed it growing up, but none spoke of it. The source was Lord Udra. Although Drakoryan brothers each father sons with an individual mate, the offspring consider them to be shared father figures. At least, it's supposed to be that way. It was different for us, however, not because Turin and I were not encouraged to look to our uncles as father figures, but because Lord Udra was always distant towards the

two of us in favor of Zyvis. Where our fathers fostered cooperation, Lord Udra fostered a competitiveness that my mother
worried would impact the bond we would need as adults. It's a
bond that is especially important now that we've taken a mate.
I feel a stab of resentment as I flex my arm. With our mate
already reeling from her own trauma, she needs the structure
of our combined strength. How can we give her that if there
are fractures in our brotherhood?

I turn my attention to Turin. His injury was minor
compared to mine. His elbow is already nearly healed. I want
to thank him for saving me, but instinct tells me not to bring
it up until we are alone. This will need to be addressed at some
point, but not now. "Father is right. You fought well. You
deserved to win."

"It's a bitter victory." Turin climbs from the pool. Isla is
afraid of me."

"She is afraid of dragons. It is not just you."

"She'd best learn to overcome that fear." Zyvis has been
eavesdropping and surprises us by finally speaking as he
emerges from the pool, his injury mended. He pulls his skirt
over his wet body.

Under the water I flex my injured arm, feeling the strength
return. I ball my fist and imagine striking his arrogant face.

"We should be patient, Zyvis." Turin arches a brow at our
younger brother. "We should remind ourselves that fear is
understandable." He pauses. "Unless it leads to an act of
cowardice."

Zyvis' face colors in anger.

I turn my attention to Turin. Although passionate, he's
also reasonable. Having made his point, he changes the
subject.

"Did our fathers say how the harvest is going?"

The diversion is an unspoken reprieve to an issue we know

will need to be addressed later. I wait to see if Zyvis accepts the uneasy truce. He does.

"Yes. They say it's going well, but with the Mystic Mountain now being guarded day and night, all Drakoryan hands are needed to have the harvest in the storehouses by week's end." Zyvis looks at his leg. The water has nearly healed it now. I think I'd have been justified in doing worse but say nothing. "Were it not for the ShadowFell," Zyvis complains, "we'd be preparing to celebrate at our leisure, not helping villagers with the harvest."

"Things are different now," Turin reminds him. "With the villagers relocated to the empire, the storehouses will need to be stocked with enough to feed everyone." He pauses. "My father says some of the villagers have asked for their own storehouse, just as they had in the villages they left."

"Their own?" Zyvis is indignant. "It is not necessary. Our storehouses can hold all we bring back and more."

"Word is that the king will likely allow it."

"Why?" Our youngest brother's voice carries through the cavern.

"Think on it, Zyvis," I snap. "They've been displaced. They grow the food and we take our portion and leave them theirs. Each village over the mountain had its own storehouse. Why shouldn't we allow them one here?"

"Why?" Zyvis repeats my question back to me. "Because we are their rulers."

"Yes, and we have always been fair." I fix him with a hard stare. "For all that has changed, our fairness should not." I flex my arm again. The pain is minimal now. I lift myself onto the ledge of the pool.

"There's another thing that hasn't changed," Turin says. "We are brothers with a mate who needs our attention. We have a joint purpose in Isla now. Her care and comfort and needs must come before all else." He looks at Zyvis. "Even before our own pride."

"Your journey on that path starts now, Turin." I clap my hand on his shoulder. "Go to her. She will never learn that dragons can be noble until we teach her."

Turin nods. "Thank you, brother."

"Zyvis," I say, "don't you want to offer Turin brotherly support as he goes to Isla?'

I don't want to command our youngest brother to do what he knows he must. I sometimes hate how much he reminds me of Lord Udra. As he mutters his begrudging congratulations, I cannot help but draw the comparison. He turns away as he says it, so we cannot see the lie in his eyes.

Eight

ISLA

I have spent the past few hours in thoughtful silence as a maid I do not need prepares me for a man I do not want. I was bathed and clad in a sheer, soft gown. My hair, unbound from its braid, has been brushed to a gleaming russet wave scented with lavender.

Afterwards, I sent Sal away. I want time to collect myself, to reflect on Lady Klea's advice. The bedchamber I've been given is in an oval room with a comfortable bed and thickly cushioned chairs. Soft woven rugs cover the stone floors. But the most impressive feature of the room is an arched window with carvings etched around the rim. It's a large window that overlooks the southern valley where residents of a dozen or more displaced villages now work to make one large one before winter.

The wind carries faint sounds of sawing and hammering, yet I await a different noise. When I hear the door behind me open, I steel myself. He has arrived, and while I do not hear

Turin's footfalls, I can feel his gaze on the rigid line of my back.

"May I enter, Isla of Branlock?"

I turn my head enough to glance at him from the side.

"Would it matter if I refused?"

He does not answer as he comes to stand beside me. I try not to think of what he can become. In the dying light, we watch two villagers struggle to erect support timbers for a cottage.

"All the villagers are here and safe," he says.

"Not all." I swallow a lump in my throat. "Not those of Branlock." I pause, pondering what my life would have been like if the ShadowFell had targeted a different village. I'd likely be among the women I watched yesterday, sitting in circles as they tied bundles of rushes into thatches for their roofs. My sister Zara would be at my side, along with the other maidens. Yes, we'd be uncertain, here in this strange land of our dragon rulers. Still, we'd have each other.

"I am alone." I speak the thought aloud and feel my face color. I sound weak, mournful. I brace myself for Turin's pity, for him to remind me that he and his brothers will be my family now. But he doesn't.

"We will avenge you, Isla. We will save your sister and the other maidens."

"You can't promise me that with certainty." I look up at him and he averts his eyes. He knows I speak the truth.

"You're right." He sighs as he concedes. "I cannot promise you with certainty. But my brothers and I come from a line of warriors. You'll not get a promise from anyone more capable of honoring it." Turin turns to me. "Isla of Branlock. Until I can fulfill your heart's desire, what can I give you to put you at ease?"

I look full into his face. The shoulder-length blonde hair is pulled into a knot at the top of his head. His features are strong and defined. His eyes are light grey with flecks of green. A short-cropped blonde beard hugs a strong jaw. My fingers twitch. I wonder if the beard is as soft as the lips I realize I'm staring at.

"What do you want?" he asks again. "Tell me, and if it is within my power to grant, you shall have it."

He is a man, beseeching a woman to tell him how to please her. Yet I know under that softness is fire that can turn him into the beast of my worst nightmares.

In that moment, I find my answer. "I want to stop being afraid," I say. "I want to be brave." I pause. "I want to know how to kill a dragon."

Turin turns away, running a hand over the curve of his bearded jaw. He crosses his arms across his broad chest as he stares down at me. I study his face, looking for signs of amusement. There is none.

"You will be a Drakoryan Bride, Isla." His tone is reasoned. "You'll have no need to be brave. We will protect you..."

"No." My heart is thudding in my chest, and even if my request is irrational, just speaking it gives me a sense of power that I've not felt since before the attack. "Your protection is irrelevant. I will never feel safe until I can feel safe alone. I cannot feel safe alone if I can't defend myself."

"Isla..." he begins.

"I want you to teach me." I raise myself to my full height, and although I am still so small compared to this huge Drakorayan warrior, I don't feel it. Both Lyla of Fra'hir and Lady Klea were right. If I am to survive, I must find my purpose, and my power. "If you don't vow to teach me, I will not lie with you."

His mouth quirks into a smile. "Is this the same water-logged waif I found floating in the ashy water of a village well?"

His grin is handsome, but I refuse to let Turin's charm do its work.

"Kneel." I speak the word earnestly. "Kneel and promise."

"Kneel?" He raises an eyebrow.

"Yes." I step back. "Kneel, Lord Turin of Za'vol. Kneel and promise, and I will put aside my pain and lie with you this night. I will accept your body, and your protection, if you are not false. I will give you my innocence if you vow to help me regain my bravery in the face of danger. You will be my first if you promise to teach me to kill a dragon."

"And what promise will you extract from my brothers?" he asks.

Now I'm the one who smiles. If this great man finds my demands amusing, he's not showing it. He is treating me as one who holds the advantage.

"That," I say, "will be between me and them."

Lord Turin holds out his hand. I stretch mine across his palm. It looks like a child's hand by comparison. He places his other hand over mine and drops slowly to one knee. Even kneeling, he is nearly eye level, this huge lord.

"Isla of Branlock," he says, "I, Turin of Za'vol, vow not only to protect you with my life, to avenge the wrong done to you and your village, to save your sister and friends if I can, but I also promise to teach you what I have taught human soldiers. I will teach you when and where a dragon is most vulnerable. I will teach you how to find its soft spots, where to best lodge a blade to bring it down. Isla of Branlock, I will teach you how to kill a dragon." He grins again, this time wickedly. "But I vow to also teach you such pleasure that you will never kill me."

I feel a tingle of desire. For the first time, I notice how beautiful he is. My heart flutters in my chest.

I have never kissed a man. My virgin lips press to his in what starts as a chaste gesture. His lips are warm and stay affixed to mine as he rises and lifts me into his hard, strong arms. He carries me as if I am a child.

"Another," he says when our lips part. I press mine to his for the second time. This time his tongue moves between them —bold, hot, demanding. I feel the faint throb between my legs. I feel...desire.

Turin lowers me to the bed I've slept on since I arrived. He undoes his leather skirt and drops it to the floor. I feel his weight dip the mattress as he joins me on the bed. I feel nervous but not afraid. I feel a quiver run through me as his body touches the length of mine. My hand is trembling as I reach up to touch his arm. His shoulder feels like a sun-warmed boulder.

Turin is quiet. He lays back, his eyes riveted on mine as my hand moves over the rise and slope of his muscles. He watches me through gray eyes that flash with gold. I swallow my rising fear. He watches me with dragon eyes, but I have his promise in my heart and am not afraid.

I sit up, trailing my hand down the ridges of his torso to the junction of his thighs, where the tower of his cock rises from a thicket of golden curls.

"What do you know of coupling, Isla of Branlock?" His voice is thick with desire. His cock bobs towards my hand, as if encouraging me to reach for it. I think of my mother, who raised me and my sisters to be of good character, and how she would chide me for my boldness. Still, I was always curious, and prone to eavesdrop on the young wives who went to the well to draw water.

"I know that is a cock." I nod towards the eager rod of flesh. "It goes between my legs. Some of the women of the village said the first time hurts." I feel my brow furrow with sudden misgiving. "Will it be worse for me? The men of my village were not so large as you, so their cocks ..."

He sits up, his eyes flashing. "What do you know of their cocks?"

I pull my hand away, angry at his tone. "Women talk. All I know I learned from listening."

Turin sighs. "Forgive me. Dragons are jealous of what is theirs." He lifts a hand to cup my face. "There may be pain, but it will be lessened if your body is properly prepared."

He raises himself to his knees. His cock juts from his groin like a fleshy sword. Turin reaches for the hem of my shift and lifts it over my head. His eyes caress my naked body. He trails a finger from the top of my shoulder downward, mimicking how I touched him. I feel a tingle along the path of his finger. The soft throb between my legs increases. I am wet.

"That feeling is your woman's desire."

I look up at him curiously. "How do you know where my desire is hidden? It is easy to see on a man."

He chuckles. "A Drakoryan's sense of smell is as strong as his sight. I can scent your sweet arousal, Isla of Branlock, the ambrosia of your honeyed musk. It's but a trickle now. Let me make it flow."

Turin wraps an arm around my waist and lowers his huge head. I feel a sudden hot, wet pressure on the right nipple of my breast. Pleasure tears through me like a spear that lodges in my quivering core. I understand now. I feel a ripple low in my belly and a steady throb that corresponds with the pulses of his mouth. The room resounds with a woman's lusty cry. I realize the cry is mine. My head is thrown back. My long hair tickles the back of my calves as I arch my body towards the huge man holding me. The pad of his forefinger slips through the seam of my pussy, stroking the swollen folds of my inner flower. At the apex of my cleft, Turin's deft touch finds a spot that has me moving hungrily and mindlessly against his hand.

I want to ask him what he is doing, but the words don't come. While the women of my village spoke of pleasure, nothing could have prepared me for this. Turin's lips press against my neck. He moves around to clutch the pale mounds of my buttocks, squeezing and spreading them. A finger slips between to caress the rosebud of my anus.

His hands are everywhere. His mouth is, too. I am helpless again as he lays me on the bed, but this is not a fight I want to win. I think of Jayx's words and realize he was right. In this moment, the burdens of my past are lifted as I find solace in pure, feral pleasure that drives everything from my mind, even if for just a moment.

Turin spreads my legs. He is between them, peering down. His finger presses against the entrance of my virgin pussy. He looks at me with slight concern. "You are well guarded here, too, my little warrior. You will have to be brave as I shatter this shield."

What does he mean? He does not give me time to question it. Turin slides between my legs. I feel the head of his cock press against the sensitive bud of flesh. It nudges and moves like a finger, hot and quivering, teasing the need from within. He takes my hand and lowers it so that I grip the length of his cock. I feel the surface change from smooth to ridged under my hand. I feel his girth diminish, compressed under my touch.

"I don't want to hurt you any more than I have to." Those are the last words he speaks before pulls both my hands above my head, before the cock teasing the tiny pleasure center of flesh slips down and slides into my need-slick pussy. My vision goes red from a sharp, unexpected pain and I scream into the mouth that has found mine.

I'm angry. I feel betrayed. He hurt me. I pull my hands from his grasp and he rises up on his arms, absorbing my pain as I pummel his chest with my clenched fists.

"Sssshhh," he says, even as he allows me to thrash him. "Wait, my little fighter. Wait."

My blows grow less violent as the pain recedes to be replaced by the soft throb that made me open my legs in the first place. Hands that struck now move to claw at his back with renewed need. I am mewling like a hungry kitten as Turin begins to move, his deep, certain laugh mingling with my animal cries of desire. There is a shadow of soreness, but it is eclipsed by the pleasure as his cock soothes me with its first strokes. I feel my hips move of their own accord, following his motions with clumsy sweetness. Turin is smiling down at me. His golden eyes are gray again, and filled with caring. I close mine, unable to take all of what he offers. It feels like too much. I am buffeted by sensations, lost as Jayx said I would be on a sea of bliss. Pleasure moves through me in a rolling rush and Turin holds me through it. Only when the last wave of ecstasy washes over me do I feel a flood of warmth as he christens my newly claimed body with his seed.

He has claimed me, this first Lord of Za'vol. He kisses me, tells me I was brave. In the light of guttering candles, I think to myself that this is just the beginning. I will be braver still.

Nine

ZYVIS

It is my mother's idea for me to help ferry villagers back across the mountain for the harvest. Her criticism is easier to take than my father's. When she came to me, I was sure she'd mention the battle. I have been wracked with shame since it ended— shame of defeat, shame of disappointing my father, shame of losing control. I failed in every conceivable way.

How can I go to Isla now? My mother seemed to know I needed to talk. In her practical way, she reminded me that one failure does not excuse another, and if I failed to find a way to woo and win Isla, my house would produce no sons to carry on after me and my brothers.

"Go to the villages with the others, Zyvis." She'd come to find me on the wall, where I'd gone to stare into the crevasse where I'd nearly killed my own brother. "It will do you no good to steep in self-loathing. Counter the error you made with an act of nobility." I'd flinched. Even if Mother did not directly mention what I did to Jayx, the reminder that she'd witnessed it deepened my shame.

"I'm not a farmer, Mother."

"Neither are the other lords. But we have relied on a share of the villagers' harvest for years to fill our storehouses. With the villagers here, the entire harvest must be brought here as well. Dragon strength is needed to take workers to the fields. Within days, sheaves of grain and baskets of grapes and berries and figs will be ready for transport. Dragons will journey to and fro with food not just for our households, but also for the villagers we are now sworn to protect. Will you stay and lick your wounds or behave as the man I raised you to be?

My mother should have been born a man. Even her quiet words command obedience.

"If it would please you, Mother," I'd said.

"My son." Despite what I'd done, she still looked at me with loving eyes. "Please me not. Please yourself. Take pleasure in doing good."

As I wing my way across the mountains, I understand the wisdom of her advice. Going to the now-abandoned village reminds me there are challenges greater than personal disappointment. I am carrying two iron cages filled with village men who will harvest the crops they left behind. My friend Zelki of Castle Fra'hir flies behind me. He also clutches two cages. The air above the mountains is bitter cold and thin. We take turns falling one behind the other to breath out warm air onto our passengers. It's the same method we used when we evacuated the villagers.

We are heading for the ruins of Stonecross. As we approach, two dragons wing back towards the empire, their cages filled with frightened livestock. Below, men work quickly with scythe to harvest and bundle wheat in the fields. The dragons who bore them have shifted back into men who work side by side with villagers to prepare the harvest for gathering.

The Drakoryans always managed how much food villages were allowed to grow, making sure they produced enough for themselves but also for us, their rulers. We kept land they weren't allowed to farm burnt to ash. Villages that pleased us were allowed to produce more to trade with one another. A village that displeased us saw more land burnt, curtailing the harvest for their use since the dragons always took their due. This system kept them obedient. Each year at harvest the crops would be bundled or put in baskets that we would come by night and take away.

The fields we pass are thick with bundled wheat and huge baskets of other crops. It's a good harvest this year. We will need it since winter is on its way. We will not be able to till fields in the Drakoryan valley before spring. What is harvested here will have to feed both villagers and Drakoryans until new fields can be planted.

As what remains of Stonecross comes into view, I glide down with Zelki. We hover above the ground outside the village, pumping our wings to slow our descent as we lower the cages full of human cargo to the ground. Once they are safely on the ashy earth, we fly a safe distance away and land ourselves. I shift into a tower of violet flame beside Zelki's blue one. Re-formed as men, we walk to the cages to free the villagers so they can work.

The men we've brought are strong from a life of toiling in the fields, toiling for us. As dragons, we are used to seeing fear in their eyes. As a Drakoryan man standing face to face with those we rule, I still see that fear. But I also see something else. Zelki sees it, too. As the villagers head to the fields to take up their scythes, he comes to stand at my side.

"They resent us now," he says.

"They shouldn't." I look over at my friend. He is the youngest of House Fra'hir but was the second to take his mate.

I don't want to think of that now. I look to the villagers. "We saved them from the ShadowFell."

"They have not forgotten what we did before we saved them." Zelki picks up the scythes and hands me one. "For now, they are too busy rebuilding and harvesting to think on it. I fear that come winter as they sit by the fire they'll stew on our deception, of how we burned their lands and took their daughters."

Two scythes lean beside what remains of a cottage. We each pick one up as we pass on the way to the fields, which are apart from the villages and blessedly undamaged by the ShadowFell's fire. I try to be optimistic. "Come winter they'll be warm and well fed in better houses than they had here. And should there be unrest, they'll have but to look to the mountain castles to remember that the dragons now watch their every move."

Zelki laughs. "Sometimes you remind me of your father. Peace through dominance, Lord Udra used to say when he was training the troops."

I frown at the mention of my father. I'd come here to forget his overbearing ways but find myself defending him. "He's right, Zelki. Are not the race of humans who serve in our army and households content?"

Zelki nods towards two villagers bundling sheaves of wheat. As they work, they look towards the empty houses that used to be their homes. "The humans who make up our serving class have been subjugated for generations. But these? They have been more independent. Yes, we ruled them, but from a distance. Yes, we were a threat, but not a daily presence. The villagers had more autonomy, more freedom. It's more than land and homes they lament."

I begin to swing my scythe, felling grain at twice the rate of the village men. Several look up to watch before going back to work. Zelki may be right. The villagers may well resent the changes in their lives. They may resent us as rulers. However, the Drakoryans will always be stronger, both in man and dragon form.

I do not want to speak on this any longer. I fall silent and concentrate on my work, cutting a swath through the field. Zelki does the same. Villagers fall in behind us, gathering the wheat to bundle into sheaves. I look back at them. They glance up but avoid meeting my gaze.

Ten

JAYX

Before everything changed, Turin's claiming of Isla would have been celebrated by a great feast. It's easy to imagine Isla walking into the room on my brother's arm, clad in the sunset orange of his dragon color. With her red hair, she'd have looked like a living flame.

The other lords would have lifted horns and goblets of our best wine as they cheered and pounded the tables. By the time Turin arrived in the hall, I'd have already been half drunk on wine and anticipation of my chance to bed our beautiful mate.

Damn the ShadowFell.

Anger flares in my breast but is cooled by the guilt I feel over indulging my self-pity. True, the Drakoryans have lost a tradition. Isla has lost far more.

Turin told me that leaving her side was nearly as difficult as winning her in battle.

"She's unbelievably sweet." My younger brother smiles at

me over the pile of food mother has ordered brought to the empty hall. "And unbelievably passionate."

"It's the red hair," I muse with a wink.

My brother grows serious. "It's more than that. There's an intensity to her, a heat." His eyes meet mine. "She made me promise her something, Jayx."

"And what was that, Turin?"

"She wants to learn to fight. She wants to learn how to kill ... a dragon."

"To kill a...to kill a *dragon*?" I repeat my brother's words back to him, sure I've misheard him. I lean back in my chair. "And of course, you told her this was impossible."

"No. I promised her I would."

"Turin." I push away from the table and stand. "Why would you make such a vow? You should have promised her anything but that."

"It's all she wanted, Jayx."

"To kill a dragon?" I throw my hands in the air and turn away.

"Look past her request, to the heart of the matter." Turin stands and follows me. "She wants to feel safe from the ShadowFell."

I whirl on him. "Making her feel safe is our job!"

"I told her that." He runs his hand through his hair and sighs. "I told her we would always protect her. But she wants to be able to protect herself."

"No maiden can kill a dragon," I say. "No single man can for that matter. It's not been done."

"Just because something hasn't been done doesn't mean it's impossible." Turin points to the scar running across my chest. "Remember when you got that?"

"It's a battle scar, and I'm not the first dragon to get a scar that didn't heal."

"True," Turin says. "But remember what your father said?"

I do. Our troops had been positioning the catapult that would hurl a huge spear at an approaching ShadowFell. I was chasing the enemy into position when it had rounded on me with surprising swiftness, sending me hurtling downward. Our soldiers had let fly with the huge spear. It had caught me diagonally across my chest. The wound was deep, and later my father told me that had it entered at an upward trajectory between the two largest scales under the edge of my wings, it would have punctured the air sacs that dragons need to survive. There are other spots, too, that we must protect. When we open our giant mouths, the venom glands are revealed. Should they be punctured we could choke on our own fire venom.

In training our human troops, we teach defensive moves, such as ducking and covering with dragon-scale shields to protect them from fire, or the use of large weaponry to fire spears at a flying or netted ShadowFell. We have never told even them that a man with a sword could run it between those scales to bring a dragon down. It is not the kind of information we want our subjects to have.

Turin is right, though. It is not impossible to kill a dragon. Still, the promise he made to Isla is fanciful.

"A maiden is not a man, Turin." I pour myself a goblet of wine.

"Then what can it hurt if I teach her sword play, or tell her where a dragon is weakest? It will avail her little other than to feel more secure. Can we deny her that?"

I take a sip of my wine. "Zyvis won't like it."

"I'd think you of all people would care the least about what Zyvis thinks." Turin pours himself a glass of wine as well. "Where is our brother, anyway?"

"Gone to help with the harvest. Mother sent him."

"Do you plan to confront him?" Turin stares at me over the rim of his cup.

"I don't know. He tried to kill me."

"Maybe Isla can slay him for you." Turin winks at me.

"That's not funny, brother," I say, but I can't stop the laugh that follows.

Turin joins me, and for the moment, all tension is forgotten. We are a third of the way to claiming our mate if we can just keep our bond while finding a way to fulfill our mate's growing passion and her desperate need to feel safe again.

Eleven

ISLA

I awake to savory and sweet aromas. Turin has had Sal lay my fireside table with such a bounty that I ask if he intends to dine with me.

"I dined with Jayx while you slept," he tells me. "But my brother's appetite is not for food."

I feel my face flood with heat at the reminder that I will soon feel the touch of a second man. Once again, I think of my mother, a meek and moral woman who taught me and my sister Zara that should we marry and endure to live faithfully with one man.

One.

What would she say if she saw me now, if she knew that within a span of days I'd be expected to spread my thighs for not a single man but three? Only the witches took lovers. We were good girls, she said. We were not witches who lived a different morality. She expected us to honor what lessons she'd taught.

"You're lost in thought." Turin's words bring me back to myself. "What furrows that pretty brow?"

He puts a plate in front of me. On it are two roasted quail drizzled with rosemary gravy, golden carrots. Beside the plate sits a bowl of brandied pears. The dinner is served with a goblet of sweet wine.

I tear a piece off the bread as I ponder my reply. "Just that I wish my mother had taught me more of what I would need to survive life's unpredictable path. She intended for me to have a single husband."

Turin leans back in his chair. "I'm sure if she'd known, she'd have prepared you for this, too."

Something occurs to me then. "The dragons that took my sister. Do they turn into men, too? Will they..."

"Isla..."

"Tell me."

I can see that he is hesitant to answer. "No," he says. "But according to the oracle, they seek humanity. It is why they took the maidens. They want ready mates when it is time."

"How would they gain humanity?"

"You are too curious."

"Tell me." I fix him with a challenging stare.

"The same way the Drakoryan did. Witch magic. Ages ago, the God and Goddess of the Wyld punished a king of men for his cruelty by turning his three sons into the first dragon men. Since then, our kind have had to balance our human side with our dragon nature. The ShadowFell seek the same magic, only to turn from dragon to human."

"Why, when dragons are more powerful?"

He smiles at this. "Because in battle, our humanity gives us the advantage. They have driven all other dragons to the other side of the world, save us. They would become like the Drakoryans, but that must not happen. They would be the cruelest of masters."

"Where do they live?" I ask.

"Deep in the shadows of the mountains. Where, we do not know."

I think on this, think on Zara sitting somewhere in the dark, chained to a wall, afraid as dragons rumble in the dark. A tear trails down my face.

"How can something inhuman tend to my sister and the others?" I ask miserably.

Turin takes my hand. "While dragons may not be humans, they are not stupid. Especially not the ShadowFell. They stole your sister and the others away. They will keep them alive. We must rescue those maidens before the dark enemy fulfills its plan."

Cruel masters. Now I think of Zara lying under some huge, dark-haired man who would take her with a primal roughness. I am wracked with guilt. I should not have hidden in that well. I should have let myself be captured so I could protect her.

Turin rises from his chair. "Eat," he says.

"I don't feel like it."

He crosses his broad arms across his chest. "Eat," he repeats. "If you don't, you won't have strength for your first lesson in swordsmanship."

I look up at him. "Are you teasing me?"

"No. But eat. Or you'll have to wait."

Turin leaves the room and I start to eat. Outside, the sun peeks through clouds. How long have I been asleep? Before I laid down, Turin told me that he would soon go help with the harvest and leave me with Jayx.

In the distance I see the shadow of a dragon returning from the fields across the mountain, a huge cage filled with men clutched in each clawed foot. I think of the golden wheat that grew so tall my sister and I would play hide-and-seek in it as children. We'd jump up, laughing as we caught sight of our cottages over the grain-laden heads. I think of those cottages now, burned to timbers, the carrion birds feeding on the charred remains of the slaughtered. I start on the quail, committed now to finishing my meal, eager for my first lesson.

I'm just finishing the last of my bread when Turin returns. My heart drops in disappointment when I see what he's holding.

"That's not a real sword." I rise and walk over to him, eyeing what looks like a child's toy.

"No, it's not." He holds out the wooden sword. "However, it was my first, and today I wield a sword better than my father ever did thanks to my early training with this one." He holds it out to me. "Master a wooden sword and I'll see a proper one forged just for you."

"A sharp one?" I take hold of the wooden sword. "Sharp enough to kill a dragon?"

"Sharp enough to make you feel safe."

It's a good enough answer.

Jayx moves behind me, lifting my arm. I look down the wooden blade, imagining it is real.

"Let us begin the lesson," he says.

Twelve

JAYX

Is this the same woman I spoke to in the fog the day before the fight? That woman seemed lost and afraid. When I walk into her bedchamber I see a different woman. Her back is to me, the bottom of her velvet green gown swishing gracefully as she moves left and right. Through the sleeves I can see the curve of her muscles as she holds up the training sword I recognize as the one Lord Egir made for Turin when he was a child not much smaller than she is now. Isla wields the weapon with as much enthusiasm as my brother ever did.

He's taught her how to hold it, to swing it with two hands. Her arms sweep to the left and then the right once, and then twice. On the third swing, she hits the side of a chair.

"God's bones," Isla mutters.

"That's language more suited to a common muckspout, not a lady."

She startles at the sound of my voice.

"Lord Jayx."

"I see Lord Turin has begun your lesson." I incline my head towards her weapon. I wait for her to put it down.

"He told you, then? What I willed from him."

I shut the door and turn back to her. "What will you from me?" I walk over to Isla. She stands her ground but does not lower the sword.

"Are you mocking me?" she asks.

"Does my brother mock you?"

"No. He knows I will not be mocked, even if I am but a village girl."

I try not to smile. Turin is right. Our mate has grown fierce. I prefer fierce to fading. I like this version of Isla much better than the one I spoke to on the misty wall.

"Lower your sword, Isla of Branlock. I've come to fuck, not to fight."

Her face colors prettily, and I notice her nipples, hard as spear points, are straining against the fabric of her bodice.

"I will not fuck until I have your vow."

I feel my cock rising against my skirt. Her brashness is exciting me in ways compliance never could. I want to push myself inside her, to embed my cock in her heat. I am already agitated by my wait, and her boldness is like a taunt.

"'Tis a dangerous game you play, little flame."

Her eyes flash with a moment of fear, yet she holds her ground in spite of it. "My circumstance is no game, Lord Jayx."

"No. No, it's not." Her words sober me. I reach out and put my hand on her sword tip, pushing it down. "What will you, from me?" I ask once more.

The tip of the wooden sword is on the floor now. She looks up at me. She's so incredibly beautiful with her wild tangle of red hair and green eyes.

"What other ways are there to fight? Besides with swords, I mean?"

I consider her question. "Well, there are bows. Zyvis is a better archer."

"What do you excel in?"

"Swordplay," I tell her.

"I have Turin for that. What else."

Imp, I think. *I should thrash her.* Instead, I smile.

"Sometimes if you cross blades your opponent disarms you. What then? Raise your sword."

She complies, and I knock it from her hand. She cries out in surprise and before she can even react, I grab her wrists. She begins to thrash and kick wildly.

"Helpless as a wee bird," I say as she struggles. Her face is flaming with rage. "Anger won't do you any good. So, *think*." I let her go. "When I grabbed your arms, you kicked. That's because I disabled the weapons of your hands and you used the only other weapons you had – your feet. A true warrior is trained to reach for another weapon as soon as his sword leaves his hand. It could be a sword on his back. It could be a knife at his side. But reach he does. He does not let the foe distract."

I stand beside her and pantomime the movement. My hand flies back as if I've been disarmed. I instantly reach over my shoulder to draw a pretend sword. I swing my arm back in an arc that flows into an imaginary uppercut. Beside me, Isla's eyes widen in admiration.

"Teach me," she says.

"I will," I tell her. "But as I said, I've another lesson for you tonight."

"And another weapon to grip?" She arches a brow.

"One night with my brother and you already adopt the manner of a doxy?"

Her face falls. "Is it wrong, then, for a woman to allow herself to be eager as a man."

I instantly regret my words. "No. I beg forgiveness, Isla of

Branlock. Your curiosity is refreshing." I pause. "And how did you find your first time with a man?"

She considers my question before answering. "In the village I heard the wives speak of bed sport. Yet, they did not describe the pleasure I felt. I think..." She pauses, thinking. "The way your brother made me feel. Is it like that for dragons when they fly, rising and falling? Blissful? Never had I thought to find such sensation while still on the ground."

I feel a sudden envy that Turin opened her eyes to the pleasure of sex, then push that envy away. I've bedded more women than he, and plan to build on the foundation he started. I think of how to best do it, of how to make Isla's experience with me just as potent, just as memorable.

"Did my brother tell you where a dragon is weak?"

"Yes." She points to a spot directly in front of my armpit and her eyes fall on my scar. I wait for her to ask how I got it, but she doesn't. "This spot, on a dragon. To pierce the sacs of air."

"Yes. And did he show you where a man is weak?" I move her hand over my heart. "Here." I press her palm to my hot chest. "Win this and he will be your slave."

"Not every man," she says, and I know she is right.

"I'm not speaking of every man now, just me. It's the two of us now, Isla. Would you let me plunge my sword into your sweet sheath? It's as hard as steel, and as eager to conquer you on a softer battlefield than the one you long for." I lift her by the waist. "Wrap your legs around me."

She obeys. Her chest is pressed against mine. I can feel the mounds of her breasts, the hard nubs of her nipples, against my skin. Her body is so close. Only a barrier of fabric separates us. I am mad with need for her. I must have her. I can wait no longer. I take her to the bed and toss her onto the mattress, falling roughly onto her. She gasps, her eyes wide. The pupils expand, leaving only a rim of emerald. Her pink lips are parted. I feel her hot breath against my face. Her dress is up around her waist. I can smell her arousal. She is excited.

"In battle, a conquering warrior earns respect." I reach for the neckline of her gown and pull. The fabric rips away so easily. I must be careful of my strength. I search her eyes for fear but see only a challenge. She slaps me hard across the face and I fist her hair, holding her head still as my mouth plunders hers. Her skin is bare beneath mine. The feel of her squirming body sends jolts of excitement through me. She bites at my shoulder, demanding a response. I rise up, pulling her with me. She hangs backwards over my arm as I latch on to a nipple, sucking hard, then harder, suckling until she screams and pulls my hair.

I dip my hand between her thighs. She's wet. She's more than wet. Her thighs are slick, and even as she struggles her hips arch towards my hand. Little minx. She is pushing me to dominate her. Her struggle is not opposition. It's a challenge. I lower her down, my teeth leaving little marks on her skin as I nip my way down the curve of her waist. When I grip her ass and plant my face between her thighs, she cries out a genuine objection.

"No!" Her tone is scandalized. "You can't... what...oooooohhhhh..."

But her surprised protest dies a fiery death in her wave of heated passion. The hands that frantically tried to push my head away are now twined in my hair, pulling me towards her as my tongue laves the silken petal of her inner flower. Her reaction tells me my brother did not ply this particular skill with her, and I am committed to pushing her to the limit. My tongue is the sword tip now, darting and stabbing at her clit until she surrenders in a hail of moans.

I am glad now that Isla is not a virgin. Having been opened, she accepts first one finger, and then two, into her tight velvety warmth. I move them in and out as my mouth latches onto her clit. Her moans become cries. I can feel her pussy clench rhythmically around my fingers, drenching them. My cock is impossibly hard, impossibly eager to replace them.

As the waves rocking her body slowly abate, I withdraw my fingers and slide my body over hers. Isla's eyes are hooded with lust. Her fair skin is flushed and glows with a sheen of sweat.

"Will you accept my sword as you did my brother's?" I'm positioned between her legs, the tip of my throbbing cock pressed against her clit. It's an exercise of restraint, but I want to give her this final gift – of power over even me.

"By the gods, yes." She speaks the words with certainty, and I sheathe myself in the tight scabbard of her pussy, emitting a primal cry at the slick, heated constriction that envelops my cock.

It is bliss, being inside her, and I'm so lost that I nearly forget to show her my own particular carnal magic. But I do, raising a ridge along my cock that stimulates a hidden internal seat of pleasure Isla didn't even know she had.

"Hold me down," she says through gritted teeth, and I grip her hands and hold them above her head. Isla strains against me as I fuck her. I can feel her excitement rising, and I know why. She is discovering her own strength and seeks to feel mine as well—strength that is now at her disposal. I am happy to show her. I press her hands into the mattress. I fuck her hard as her eyes lock on mine. I will leave her sore; I believe she will like that, too.

She comes, her climax milking my cock in a cadence of contractions that draw forth my seed. The release marks the most pleasurable of my life. Once a Drakoryan male takes a true mate, his desire is for no other. I know as I come that no woman has ever pleased me like Isla, my fiery warrior, my perfect flame. I'd sought to put my mark on her, but she has surely marked me as well.

Thirteen

ISLA

Jayx takes me to the pools. More accurately, he carries me to the pools. I allow myself to relax in his strong arms, because I know he is true. He has offered me his protection and made the same vow as his brother to teach me how to best protect myself. I am surrounded by strength, even as I find my own.

When I think of what I've suffered, I still feel the wound in my heart open and bleed. It would be easy to lie down and let my seeping grief drain me of the will to carry on. I am beginning to see that Lady Lyla was right. Perhaps there was some providence to my having survived. Perhaps the fate that had Turin snatch me from that well and bring me here as mate to him and his brothers is shaping a future that will reunite me with my sister.

I sigh with relief as Turin lowers my love-bruised body into the healing waters. He explains that this is where he and his brothers came to heal after the battle I witnessed from the wall. I lean back, watching the steam rise around me as I recall that awful competition.

"The combat was far more brutal than I thought it would be," I confide. "I was afraid Zyvis was going to drive you into the rocks."

I look over, noting tension in Jayx's jaw.

"Can a dragon fall to its death?" I ask.

"Yes."

"You could have died fighting for me?" The thought upsets me, and it occurs to me how much I'm coming to care for Jayx, and for Turin. While Zyvis has been kind to me since my arrival, the fact that he could have dashed Jayx to his death is unsettling.

"I didn't die." Jayx turns to me and smiles. "I'm alive, with you. And that's all that matters. The battle is best put behind us."

I nod. I am new to the ways of the Drakoryans. If Jayx doesn't want to relive the battle, there must be a reason.

"What is Zyvis like?" I turn my thoughts to the remaining brother who will bed me.

Jayx removes his skirt and slips into the pool with me. He's told me that some of the pools are stronger than others and has taken me to the weakest one. I already feel better. The water feels so good; it feels even better when he pulls me to him.

"I don't want to talk about my brother when you're naked in my arms. It's difficult enough to think of leaving to bring in the harvest tomorrow, of knowing once we return, he will take my place in your bed."

His huge hands slide down to cup my ass and I wrap my legs around his waist, my soft inner thighs pressing against the hard muscles of his torso. The steam from the pool has dampened his hair, causing it to curl slightly in the moist heat. I feel his cock enter me from below, the surface of it changing from smooth to knobby, the textured surface rippling inside me to create sensations that are different from what I experienced in the bedchamber. Jayx fucks me slowly. I whimper as his girth increases, stretching and filling me.

I lean forward and bite his shoulder. His skin is warm and salty. I break my grip and cry out when he pushes his finger against my bottom hole.

"Jayx!" I try to wriggle away, but his cock is lodged so tightly inside me that it holds me fast. I'm locked onto him, and he's smiling wickedly as his persistent finger breaches the defensive ring of muscle and finds its way inside.

"New pleasures," he says, fucking my ass with his finger as his cock begins to pulse. It feels so wanton, riding the swell of *this* pleasure. Yet I cannot stop. Passion rises in me like lava and erupts. It ripples through me as Jayx joins me in mutual climax.

I cling to him, thinking how just a day ago I could not imagine letting myself experience such closeness with a second man. I close my eyes and lean my head on Jayx's shoulder. He strokes my hair. I know he fears the moment I go to his last brother. I fear it, too, although I don't know why.

He lifts me from the water and sets me on the edge, settling beside me. There's a bowl of candied fruit between us. I pick a piece and bite down, enjoying the burst of sweetness on my tongue. I'm still getting used to the variety of food at the castle.

As if sensing my thoughts, Jayx nods towards the morsel in my hand.

"While I am glad we were allowed to take you as a War Bride, I do wish you'd been able to enjoy the feasts that come with claiming day. When this is all over—when we have defeated the ShadowFell once and for all— we will celebrate our victory, and then hold a special feast just to honor you."

He shifts towards me, a wistful smile on his face. "You'll

love it, Isla. Whole roasted boars stuffed with apples and plums —their skins rubbed with exotic spices—geese, pheasant, more fruits than you can identify. Each village grows a different kind of food. You'll see when we bring the harvest in tomorrow." He balls his fist. "Berries as big as your hand. Melons with juices that increase passion or prolong the act of love. Pastries, cakes..."

"We never feasted like that in the village." I cut him off. Then he looks away as he realizes he has been describing the privilege of rulers to a woman whose village supplied what his kind has forced us to grow.

"Isla. You're one of us now," he says. "Once Zyvis takes you, once we are bonded, you'll be the Lady of Za'vol."

"Do you think it will be so easy?" I ask.

"You will manage." He pushes a strand of hair away from my face. "Just as my mother did, just as other Drakoryan brides have done."

"It's different for me." I stand and reach for the sheet Jayx wrapped me in before we left the chamber. I wrap it around myself once more before facing him. "The other women were taken away from village life. It's easy to forget who you are when you no longer see it. Yet each day, I look out to see the villages from my window."

He stands. "But for Branlock. It is no more."

"It doesn't matter." I shake my head. "A village is a village. We all grew up with the same rules, the same structure, the same...fear. Fear of your kind." I pause. "I feel like a traitor, living here in this castle while all those villagers huddle in wind-battered tents until their homes are built."

"Before our kind, kings of men took women from the villages; it was considered an honor."

"Is it really that hard for you to understand that a family would find it easier to give a daughter to a man than to a half-dragon?" I sigh in frustration, then soften my tone. "I did not think it would be so, but I believe I can love you, Lord Jayx of Za'vol. And I can love Turin, too. I hope I will be able to love Zyvis. But I will not pretend my old life did not exist."

He smiles. "You sound like Lady Lyla of Fra'hir."

"How so?" I cock my head.

"Tythos said she remained loyal to her kin as well. I think this loyalty is a good trait. It shows your strength."

I stand on my tiptoes and kiss him. "I am glad it pleases you, my lord. For I plan to become even stronger."

Fourteen

ZYVIS

It is the day of the harvest. Tonight, after the last of the baskets of grain and fruit have been brought over the mountains I will lie with Isla.

A Drakoryan's urge to couple is strong. For the last brother to mate, the wait can be painful. The harvest has provided not only a distraction, but an outlet for the heat and energy that has been building inside me since the day of my failed attempt to best my brothers.

"It's a fair day. Good for the harvest." Jayx appears at my side. He looks relaxed and happy. He was with her last night. I feel a bubble of jealousy rise within me and look away so he doesn't see the resentment in my eyes. His very presence reminds me not only of my defeat, but of my shame in having lost control of myself in battle. Jayx has not mentioned it. I should be relieved, yet his mercy in this matter makes me feel even weaker by comparison.

Turin walks over to clap us both on the back. "Harvest

day!" He's grinning broadly and like our other mated brother, looks cheerful and at ease. "By nightfall, our storehouses will be full, and there will be enough to fill the villagers' storehouse as well. This winter will find us all well-fed."

"I told Isla once the ShadowFell are defeated, we will hold a feast to honor her," Jayx says. "A feast worthy of the most beautiful bride in all the Drakoryan Empire."

"We can't defeat them until we find them," I remind my brothers.

"With villages full of maidens and the Mystic Mountain under our constant watch, we won't have to find them." Jayx's tone is certain. "They'll come to us. And when they do, we will destroy the ShadowFell once and for all."

The other dragon lords have gathered. We are standing in the valley in an open space beyond the growing settlement. The villagers, who are working to complete the nearly finished storehouse, stop to watch us change into the very dragons that used to terrify them when they lived across the mountains. Today we will not be coming not to take their harvest, to deliver it. I think of what Zelki said when we were in the fields. If he is right, seeing their own storehouse filled with food should soothe some of the anger.

We burst into towers of colorful flame as we shift into our dragon forms. Clouds of dust stirred from our mighty wings billow from the ground as we rise into the air. The air that greets us at the edge of the valley is cold. There is already snow on the south-facing slopes, portending a harsh winter. While Drakoryans can handle the cold as both man and dragon, we prefer warmth. We spend much of the winter feasting in the hall as massive logs crackle in huge stone fireplaces.

This winter, we will have Isla to warm our beds on those long nights. I pump my wings harder, eager to get across the mountains, gather the harvest and return to Castle Za'vol, to mate with Isla and once again feel equal with my brothers.

We fly on, the wind at our backs making the journey an effortless one. As we crest the highest ridge on the range that separates the Drakoryan valley from the villages on the other side, the wind shifts. We are flying into it now.

I hear Jayx's voice in my head. *Brothers* ... The word is weighted with concern. I do not have to ask him what worries him. The wind carries a scent from over the mountains—faint but unmistakable. It is the smell of smoke. The other dragons smell it, too. I look left and right to see their yellow eyes scanning the horizon. Their voices rumble in my head.

No, they are saying. *No.*

We fly faster, beating our huge wings hard against the wind. There is no mistaking the smell as we near the end of the range where mountains give way to hills. The sense of dread increases the closer we get to the first village.

What we see is as shocking as the cold wind, and as bitter. The ShadowFell have returned to burn Stonecross. But it's not just the buildings they destroyed. The harvest is burnt, too, the brimming baskets of grain and fruit and vegetables reduced to piles of ash. Columns of smoke rising in the distance reveal that this is not an isolated attack.

Beside me, Jayx roars in anger, a cry echoed by other dragons as we split up to fly to different villages, where our worst fears are confirmed. Not a head of grain remains. Not a grape. Not a turnip. We fly around, circling like carrion birds until we land amid the ruins of villages that once fed us. The air whipping around us feels colder now, the wind more ominous.

My brothers and I have landed in Branlock, where Turin found and rescued Isla. Ironically, while this village had been burned first, the dragons that stole away the maidens and killed all the villagers save for Isla had left the crops. That they return to burn all that we harvested only magnifies the intent.

"This is dire." I glance over at my brothers.

"Dire may not be strong enough a word." Turin's eyes scan the devastation, falling on what was once a mature grove of olive trees. All that remains now are smoldering black nubs on ground burnt to the bedrock. This act of sabotage was carried out with savage glee.

"This is the work of more than one dragon." Jayx squints his eyes in the haze of drifting smoke.

"Far more," I agree. "And look..." I point to crisscrossed burn marks on earth outside the village. Not all the attacks were accurate. Those remind me of the trails we would leave when we were just learning to direct our flame."

"It hardly matters," Turin says bitterly. He's picked up the blade of a scythe, all that remains of the tool now that the handle has been burned away. In a gesture of frustration, he hurls it away. We watch it land among the rubble of a cottage. "Their aim was true enough."

We hear a rush of wind and turn to see three dragons of green, blue and gold winging towards us. They drop down and shift into the human form of our closest friends and allies. The brothers of House Fra'hir — Drorgros, Tythos, Imryth, and Zelki— walk towards us, their grim expressions mirroring our own.

"All gone." Drorgros puts his hands on his hips. He shakes his head. "We should have brought the harvest back with us each day rather than waiting to gather it all at once."

"It was impossible," Jayx replies. "We were transporting villagers back and forth in our haste to gather the harvest ahead of the cold. With the village houses destroyed, they had no shelter." His voice trails away. He's not the only one second-guessing our strategy now. We all are. When the ShadowFell returned to find the villages empty, they'd burned the buildings.

"Imryth..." I turn to the middle Lord of Fra'hir. The most

scholarly, he has studied the ShadowFell more than the rest of us. "What do you make of this?"

"That this is a different ShadowFell than we have fought before, one as calculating as it is visceral." He furrows his brow. "This destruction serves a larger purpose, and they know it. They could have burned the harvest along with the villages. Instead, they deliberately waited until Drakoryans and humans had toiled to bring in the harvest before destroying all we had accomplished."

"So, they wanted to deprive us of food to feed the villagers," I say.

"It's more than that," Imryth replies. "There was another purpose in mind, to sow discord among us and the villagers we protect." He turns to us. "How safe will they feel if we couldn't even protect their crops?"

Fifteen

TURIN

Despite what he's done, it's hard not to feel pity for Zyvis. He'd expected to come home to Isla, not turmoil. But that's what awaits us.

We return to find that the villagers have finished the storehouse that will now stand empty. They have resumed working on their cottages, but stop working as we approach, no doubt puzzled to see us flying back earlier than expected, then more puzzled still to see we carry no baskets.

Drorgros of Fra'hir is first to land. He is shifting as Jayx and I touch down and transform back to human form. As other dragons land and change, a villager named Releg approaches us, flanked by a group of other men who'd helped gather the crops.

A refugee from the village of Dalry, Releg could easily be mistaken for a dragon lord himself given his unusual size. He nearly stands eye level to me. Were I not Drakoryan, I would fear this man with the bald head and heavy brow. Releg comes to the empire having lost more than his home. He was a man of influence in Darly, which was the largest village over the mountains. It was also the wealthiest, having produced the most variety of food. His people worked hard to grow it, and this year the crops had been bountiful.

"Where is the harvest?" His voice is gruff, his tone mistrustful.

The last of the Drakoryan have changed. The Lords of Fra'hir are at our side now, the other lords behind us. We Drakoryans face the villagers. There are more of them than there are of us.

"Well?" Releg steps towards us. "Where is the food?"

"Burnt," Drorgros says. "By the ShadowFell."

A muscle in Releg's grizzled jaw twitches. He looks past us at the other lords, then back at Drorgros of Fra'hir. "By the ShadowFell?" He tilts his chin upward, clenching meaty fists at his side. "Those...terrible dragons you *claim* destroyed Branlock and Kenrick then returned to burn our houses after finding them empty?"

"There is no *claiming*." Drorgros keeps calm. "It is truth, Releg of Darly. They came in the night and burnt the harvest." He pauses. "All of it."

Releg stares at Drorgros. His boldness is infectious. The men behind him are staring us down, too. "Is there no food in this place you've brought us to?" He asks the question loudly, his voice carrying to those behind him, who begin to grumble.

"There is still food." I join the conversation, not wanting Drorgros to bear the entire burden of the villagers' anger. "Our storehouses are well stocked. If we ration..."

"So the only food in the Drakoryan Empire is in the lords' storehouses? What of our storehouses?" Behind Releg, discontent ripples through the crowd like a wave.

"We cannot help what happened," Drorgros raises his voice so that it carries above the buzzing of the agitated villagers. "Had the ShadowFell not destroyed the harvest, a portion would have been put in your storehouse."

"They are false!" From somewhere in the crowd, a voice emboldened by anonymity cries out.

"We are not false!" Jayx steps forward, composed but obviously angrier than Drorgros. He points back towards the mountains. "We are your protectors, not your enemy. Your enemy is out there—the black ShadowFell dragons who burned your crops and took the maidens of Kenrick and Branlock!"

Releg sneers. "ShadowFell? We've never seen these black dragons." His eyes rake over us with disdain. "The only dragons we've seen are the ones who change into the men standing before us...those are the only ones we've seen take our daughters." He glares at us. "And now they steal our food!" He turns back to the crowd. "Be not deceived by this trickery! They have hidden the harvest! They keep it for themselves."

"We have not!" Drorgros raises his arms, appealing for calm. Resentment settles over the crowd like smoke. "And the ShadowFell dragons do exist. There was a survivor in Branlock. A maiden. She can attest to it! She—"

Drorgros doesn't get a chance to finish his sentence. What happens next occurs without warning and stands to change everything for the worse.

Damn Zyvis and his temper! His violet flame flares high in the air, and the dragon that he becomes lets out a roar that sends the villagers fleeing in terror. He flicks his tail around to sweep Releg's legs out from under him. The leader of the angry refugees suddenly looks small where he lays on his back, staring up in terror at the dragon massive head looming over him. Zyvis' throat rumbles with a deep, reverberating growl.

"Brother!" I call to him, unsettled by what I see. Had we known what we would find today, I would not have brought Zyvis. His blood already runs hot with lust that has made him easily agitated. For a Drakoryan who has always struggled with control, his current state combined with the villager's challenge made it too easy to change.

I consider whether to change and challenge him. Both sides are watching now. I glance at Drorgros, and know he shares my fear that Zyvis may kill Releg.

Brother! I call to him with my mind, hearing my other brothers call him as well. But he is oblivious to us. His golden eyes narrow, his nostrils lengthen and flare above the ridged lip that pulls away from massive teeth. Screams of terror ring through the crowds.

HALT! The message is intended for Zyvis, yet every Drakoryan hears it. It is a familiar voice, one we have not heard for many, many years— a voice most haven't heard since the last battle of the ShadowFell.

It is the voice of our King.

Sixteen

ISLA

I was staring out the window of my bedchamber when the first dragons appeared over the horizon. I'd tried to have a rest, but nervousness about the night ahead with the last lord of Za'vol had made sleep impossible. The wind was carrying the sounds of hammering to my very window, so I'd risen to watch. The sounds of construction stopped when the villagers caught sight of what I'd noticed. Even from the distance I could see that the dragons winging their way over the valley carried no baskets.

A feeling came over me, one I'd had before but had forgotten. It was a feeling I'd had just before the ShadowFell had come to slaughter and steal. I'd not been able to sleep then, either, and had left my bed with an uneasy feeling. I'd gone out to make water but had done so with a fluttering heart although I'd told myself there was no cause for nervousness on such a beautiful night. The night did not stay beautiful for long. What had followed was blood, fire, death and the sense of loss I still wear like a veil.

The familiar quickening in my chest increases as the dragons draw closer to the settlement. Men are dropping their tools, walking away from the cottages they've been working night and day to finish. I see them look to the dragons and then to one another as they head towards an open area where the dragons are beginning to set down.

I recognize the Lords of Za'vol by their dragon colors. Turin is at the fore of the group with one of the Lords of Fra'hir. Were I not so unsettled by a growing, unexplainable feeling of dread, I would marvel at the sight of so many colorful flames erupting where the dragons land to transform. Even from here, I can sense tension between the villagers and their Drakoryan rulers. Turin and Drorgros are face to face with a large man and although I cannot hear them, I know the exchange is an angry one. And I know why. The dragons have returned empty-handed. Something has happened to the harvest. Something bad.

Now the wind carries raised voices to my window. My unease grows, but I tell myself that whatever has gone wrong, the Drakoryan will find a way to fix it. Jayx and Turin have allowed me to believe this, to believe in the power of their strength, their protection. Then it happens— a bolt of violet flame shoots upward to become a huge dragon – Zyvis' dragon. The villagers scatter, crying in collective fear. The large man has fallen and Zyvis' massive horned head hovers above him. I hear another scream.

It is my own.

I have felt this villager's fear. I have seen the beast in its most menacing form. I have looked upon it and wondered if I would live or die. I have felt its power to slaughter and steal all that I love. I slump to the floor from my window seat and clutch my hand over my ears. I am shaking. Sickness washes over me in waves and I struggle to keep down the food I'd earlier eaten.

I lay down on the floor, curling into myself. The Wolven-skin rug is warm under my cheek. I squeeze my eyes shut tight, trying to control the shudders that wrack my body, but cannot stop what enters my mind. I see the ShadowFell dragon. I see Zyvis looming over the village man. And then, in my memory, they become the same. Everything goes black.

Seventeen

ZYVIS

I'd only thought to stop them from defying their rulers. The villager was arrogant, argumentative. He dared accuse us — the noble Drakoryan— of being false. I did what needed to be done. I did what my father would have done. I'd reminded them who we were.

Would I have killed the man whose rank scent of sweat and fear filled my nose? He wasn't so bold then, cowering on the ground. I considered it, feeling the pressure of rage edging away the humanity that called for restraint.

Then I'd heard the voice of King Vukurcis, the authority sharp and commanding. It was as if a spike had been run through me, sending me backwards as I spontaneously shifted back into my human form. Once I'd turned, I realized I was not the only one who'd heard the call. My brothers and the other lords had heard it, too.

Drorgros had walked past me to extend his hand to Releg, who still lay on his back. The villager's face was ashen, his large chest still heaving in fear. He'd refused Drorgros' offer of help as he'd scrambled shakily to his feet. The villagers had moved away then as a wave, casting backwards look of resentment.

When I looked to my brothers, I saw no understanding in their faces, nor from the other lords. They all looked on me with judgmental disdain. I would answer for what I did, but at that moment, they were more focused on the voice of the king. The message to halt was not the only thing he'd spoken. He'd also commanded us gather our ladies and come to his castle. A War Council was being called.

The Drakoryan Empire is not like the kingdoms of men. The lords have their own agency and the king is a figurehead who oversees but seldom interferes, save for issues that impact the safety of the realm. His mind is bonded to every Drakoryan, and the king saves his voice, speaking only when necessary.

When the call is given, we instantly obey, for King Vukurcis is more than respected. He is legend both in strength and wisdom. He has ruled longer than any king, having fought his brothers for the right in a battle of great magnificence after the death of own father. He has outlived his brothers, the crown Drakoryan princes, and his queen. Today, he quietly resides with his sons in his Mountain of Kings which sits in the shadow of the Mystic Mountain.

As we head for home to prepare for the journey, my brothers are silent. They have closed their minds to me. They do not look at me as we fly. Even if they did try to communicate, I am in no mood. We will be required to leave for council immediately. That means I will not lie with Isla tonight. I pay for my actions with the ongoing pain of unfulfilled need.

We land on the flanking wall together. Jayx leads the way into the tunnel heading to the hall where my brothers will have no choice but to talk to me. I fight to calm myself. We have been summoned by the king and I know now is not the time to indulge my wounded pride.

We do not make it to the hall, however. We are intercepted by Isla's maid, Sal, who rushes to us in tears.

"My lords! My lords!" She wrings her hands in desperation.

Turin exchanges worried glances with Jayx. "What is wrong?"

"It's your mate, Isla. Something is amiss!"

No more needs to be said. Sal leads the way to the bedchamber. Turin is the first to burst through the door. Isla is lying on her side, her red hair fanning about her prone body. Her face is ghostly pale. He scoops her up and sits on the bed as we hover around.

"Isla. Isla." Jayx kneels, calling her name. I kneel, too, holding my breath. Her eyelids flutter and open.

"My lord Turin," she says.

"Are you ill? What happened?" He looks her over, as if searching for a wound.

"No." She sits up slowly. "I was looking out the window, to see...the dragons came in and landed. I saw them turn back to men and then..." Isla's words falter, as if she's trying to recover the memory. Then she looks to me and her countenance changes. Fear fills her green eyes.

"Leave," she says, clinging to Turin's chest like a frightened child. "Leave!!!"

I stare at her, speechless.

"Leave!" She buries her face in Turin's chest. My brothers are staring at me. I look to Jayx, who is shaking his head.

"She saw, you fool."

I stand slowly, glancing towards the window. From here I can see the settlements and the field upon which we landed. I look back at my brothers. Turin is holding Isla in a protective embrace while Jayx strokes her back. I feel like an outsider.

"Leave." It's Turin who speaks the word now. I back away and then storm from the room, hot with anger. I race through the castle, back to the ledge, bursting into flame just as I exit the tunnel. I keep to the west side of the castle where no one can see me and scream my fury into mist until I can scream no more.

Eighteen

ISLA

"I am sorry, Isla. I am sorry to ask this of you. But there is no choice."

I absorb Jayx's words as I slowly recover from the terror that overcame me. It was Turin's gesture that helped me the most. Once Zyvis had left the room, he'd fetched the wooden sword for me to hold. He'd reminded me that I was not just any mate, but a War Bride, and that I would need to be strong if I were to survive.

I'd felt ashamed of having given into panic, yet these lords would not listen to my embarrassed apologies. They told me they'd understood, and that the fault was not mine. I could tell that whatever happened with Zyvis had angered them as much as it frightened me, but they did not mention it. They only told me that the harvest had been burnt and a War Council had been called. The lords of every castle and their ladies were expected to attend, even me.

"I am not yet your lady," I'd told them.

"No, but you may not ever be if we do not go." Jayx had looked over at Turin nervously before fixing his eyes back on me. "Isla of Branlock, you must at least stay in the company of Zyvis for now. You must find a way be at ease with him." I could see the concern in his eyes. "If you do not mate with all, then you will be the mate of none."

All or none.

What does this mean for me? If I do not mate, will they turn me out? Abandon me? I do not ask, for I am thinking now of what it will mean for Turin and Jayx. I have learned that Drakoryan brothers only get one chance to mate. If it fails, their bloodline ends. In most cases, the emptiness shortens their lives, the unspent energy they'd given to a mate burning and weakening them. I care for Turin and Jayx. But Zyvis? I do not know if I can care for the brother whose dragon ire is all too familiar.

And what of their relationship with each other? When it comes time to leave for the king's castle, Turin ushers me into an enclosed litter that will be carried by Jayx. I overhear him ask Jayx whether he has seen Zyvis. Jayx tells him not to worry. Zyvis will come; he's sure of it, for no Drakoryan ignores a summon to the king's council.

"I'll not waste time chasing him down," he growls as I settle in the litter. The door shuts and I hear the whoosh of flames outside as the two Lords of Za'vol shift. The inside of the litter is plush, and across from me, Sal is both excited and nervous about her journey.

I am increasingly grateful for her now. She'd helped me don the gown I'm wearing for the journey — a plain but beautiful sky-blue dress with bell-shaped sleeves trimmed in soft ivory silk. The skirt is split to reveal an underskirt of the same ivory fabric. The scalloped neckline is just low enough to reveal the upper swell of my breasts.

She trained my thick red tresses into two thin braids that

joined in the back. The rest of my hair hangs loose around the fur collar of my traveling cloak.

"Are you well, my lady?" Sal asks, using the title I have not yet earned. I smile at her. She has been worried for me since she found me collapsed in my bedchamber.

I manage a smile. "I am fine," I say with more confidence than I feel. In truth, I am overwhelmed, and the only thing that keeps my panic in check is looking at the trunk sitting on the floor of my litter. My clothing is in there, but also the little wooden training sword that gives me a strange sort of confidence for what it represents.

I feel my stomach drop as the litter is borne into the air. Sal clutches the side, her eyes wide as she peers out the tiny window to watch Mount Za'vol rapidly recede into the distance as we head towards the Mountain of Kings.

I wish I could see the trip with the same adventurous spirit as my maid, but I have seen the reason behind the journey. One ShadowFell destroyed my village in a matter of minutes. I can barely comprehend a war, with the constant threat of attack.

The litter rises and dips. Occasionally, I feel a warm blast of air from outside, exhaled by another dragon flying in our wake. The rise and fall of the litter makes me dizzy. I find myself dozing. How long I sleep, I do not know. When I awaken, it is to the excited voice of my maid.

"Lady, there are more!" I turn my sleepy gaze to the small window by Sal, who peers out while clutching her thick brown cloak around her sturdy body. Other dragons fly past, some carrying litters similar to mine. "Come look!" Sal moves over, and I join her on the little bench on her side of the litter, taking advantage of the view. We are in the northern part of the empire. There are more trees here. The dark forest is beyond, the two mountains rising from its edge. I hear the rush of dragon wings as we head between the two mountains, dropping lower and lower. Then all goes dark and Sal and I grip the bars by the seats as we feel the litter rise rapidly through inky blackness.

I tell Sal not to panic, for Turin warned me of this. He said both the King's Mountain and the Mystic Mountain have hidden entrances known only to the Drakoryan. We are flying upwards through a vertical tunnel we entered near the base.

We are traveling fast, the wind whooshing past us. I lean back against the seat, holding Sal's hand to comfort her just as a golden light comes streaming through the window of the litter. Still clutching the bar with one hand and my maid's hand with the other, I lean forward and gasp at what I see. We are in a massive cavern with gold-gilded walls. Down below, dragons are carefully depositing other litters onto an obsidian floor. Dragons not carrying litters fly to huge ledges connected to one another and then the floor by obsidian staircases. Huge braziers blaze with flames that both warm and light the enormous cavern.

I am in awe.

There's a soft jolt as our litter lands on the floor of the cavern. I hear a *whoosh* of flame and then Turin is standing there in human form, opening the door of the litter and extending his hand to help me out

Sal emerges behind me. "Such wonders!"

I am as awed as my maid. Above us, multi-colored dragons sit on golden ledges. They shift into bright flames. The men they become head down the black staircases to the lower level. Around us, other women emerge from litters. Drakoryan Brides. I stare at them. They are beautiful and cast loving glances at the dragon lords who bore them here. I catch sight of Lord Imryth assisting Lady Lyla of Fra'hir from her litter. She turns and sees me, then says something to her mate before leaving him to walk over.

"Isla of Branlock!" She smiles warmly and extends her hands.

"Lady Lyla." I place my hands in hers and she leans forward to plant a light kiss on my cheek before standing back to study me for a moment. "Lord Turin." She turns her attention to him. "Let me see Isla to the ladies' quarters. I'm sure she'll appreciate a chance to take her ease before she sees the king."

Sees the king? I don't have time to question this before being whisked away. I glance back to see a violet dragon light on ledge above. Zyvis has arrived, just as his brother said he would, but I have no time to stop and stare. I am swept along now in a tide of other women who move towards a long, lighted tunnel.

I have only seen two castles in the Drakoryan Empire—Castle Fra'hir and Castle Za'vol. I wasn't at the first one long and was so numb from the shock of what I'd been through that I didn't have a mind to absorb the splendor. I've become accustomed to grandeur at Castle Za'vol, where I have spent time strolling in the company of dragon lords who sought to woo me. I've marveled at its massive feast hall, council room, library, and winding tunnels that open to balconies offering stunning vistas.

Yet this castle is beyond my imaginings. In the other castles, the tunnels are bare rock, narrow and dark. The tunnels here are wider and lit by ornate iron braziers. The firelight casts a glow on gems imbedded in the rock walls, which gleam with veins of gold.

As we walk, Lyla tells me that this was the first mountains settled by the Drakoryans, that the sons of King Eknor—Arok, Dax, and Yrn—battled to decide who would become the first king to rule here. King Arok prevailed, and as we pass through a room that connects two tunnels, Lyla gestures to a huge mural.

I stand and stare. I do not have to ask who it depicts. The Drakoryans are all similar in their muscular build, sharp features, and piercing eyes. The first Drakoryan king, Arok, stares down at us. The crown he wears is iron and peaked downward at the front. The three spikes rising from the band — one on the front and two on the side — are each embedded with a different color jewel — diamond, citrine, and amethyst — intended to represent the colors of the first dragons.

King Arok is flanked by his brothers, the princes, who wear smaller crowns. On the other side of the room is another second mural depicting King Arok, his brothers, and a beautiful woman with a delicate golden circlet crowning her head of white-blonde hair. This is Genev, she tells me, the first of the Drakoryan queens, the first to be claimed after the humans were conquered.

"Even a king shares his mate?" I ask.

"Yes. And no greater story exists than the claiming of the first Drakoryan queen." Lady Lyla smiles enigmatically. "But that is a tale for another day. Come along."

It is hard to drag my eyes away. Perhaps it is a trick of light, but the queen's eyes seem to follow me as I walk. The sensation is unnerving.

The second tunnel we enter is flanked on one side by solid wall and the others by pillars. Beyond them is a cavern with walls of pure amethyst. Pools of turquoise water produce tendrils of iridescent steam.

"The baths," Lyla says. "It is said they soothe not just wounds of the body, but wounds of the heart, if the God and Goddess will it."

"They are that strong?"

"Only the pools of the Mystic Mountain are stronger."

Around us, other Drakoryan brides exclaim at what they see. I turn to Lyla. "Have you been here before?"

"No," she says. "Most of us have not, save the older

brides who attended the last king's council, and that was many years ago. But a bonded bride shares some of her mates' strongest memories, be they good or bad. And no Drakoryan male's memory is stronger than his first visit to the Mountain of Kings. They are taken after their first shifting, to swear fealty to the king who sits on the throne, and to the empire."

"I have not yet bonded," I tell her.

"I know." She casts me a concerned look. "That is one of the reasons I came to fetch you away, Isla of Branlock. We need to talk."

Other women walk past us, chatting as they go. Despite the seriousness behind the gathering, they seem happy to see one another. I think of my sister, imagine her huddling somewhere dark and scary while I enjoy this splendor, and feel guilt wash over me.

I look back, searching for Sal. She is walking with several other maids, all dragging trunks similar to mine. The tunnel turns left and opens into a huge room with walls of silvery-gray stone. Carved pillars run from the marble floors to an intricate stone lattice canopy. Above the lattice is a domed roof of obsidian studded with diamonds that glitter like stars.

There are dome-shaped doorways off the main room that lead to other rooms. I watch as the women begin to head in different directions towards what I assume are the quarters.

"These are the queen's chambers," Lyla tells me. "She died before the last ShadowFell war. There will not be another until King Vukurcis joins her and one of his sons assumes the rule. Whoever wins the kingship shall be the first to take her." She takes my hand. "This way."

We head to the right and walk through one of the doorways. The voices of other women float through the space around me.

"When there is a queen in residence, she holds court here

twice a year," Lyla says. "It is said to be the grandest of affairs." She stops in front of a huge oak door. "Ah, this seems empty."

We walk into a beautiful round room. Compared to the queen's chamber, it is simple. Yet it is still elegant, with a large bed, its posts each topped with a carved dragon head. Sheer burgundy fabric runs through the mouth of each dragon, draping halfway down the posts. A coverlet of the same hue graces the thick feather mattress.

Sal has walked in, her mouth agape. "Never did I think to see such," she mutters as she hauls the trunk to a towering wardrobe fashioned with the same dragon heads carved on the door. As she snaps open the lid, my eyes fall on the sword. I look up to see that Lyla has caught sight of it as well.

I flush. "Turin gave it to me."

Lyla smiles. "No need to explain. Imyrth gave me a shield." She arches a brow. "It saved my life." She puts a hand on my shoulder. "Let's have a word." She guides me to a large cushioned window seat that does not overlook the outside, but another cave, the floor gleaming with some kind of shining gems I cannot identify.

"Isla." The seriousness of her tone gets my attention. "I wanted to get you alone, to warn you."

"About what?"

"Dismiss your maid, and I shall tell you."

"Sal, that will be all for now," I say.

"Where will I go, lady?"

"There is a special room farther down where the maids gather. There is food and drink," Lyla tells her. "My maid, Beti is there, should you seek a friend. Tell her I sent you to find her." Sal curtsies and leaves. When the door shuts behind her, Lyla turns back to me.

"You are aware of the situation?"

I nod. "I know the ShadowFell burned the harvest."

"Are you aware of what happened next? The lords talk of nothing else."

I sigh. "Zyvis. I am not only aware. I saw it."

Lyla shakes her head. "I was hoping you had not." She stands up. "Zyvis lost more than just his control. The Drakoryan Lords fear they have now lost the trust of the villagers, and under the worst possible circumstances. We face two enemies now—the ShadowFell hunger for revenge but also the very real hunger that pits man against man under the best of circumstances. Drorgros and the others had sought to reason with the villagers, to convince them that the destruction of the harvest was more reason than ever to unite for a common cause of survival. In one moment of rage, Zyvis changed all that. He has made the villagers fear the Drakoryan more than ever."

I turn away, tears spilling down my face. Lyla comes to sit beside me.

"I understand how they feel," I tell her. "And while my problems are small compared to those of the kingdom, I am almost certain that even if the empire prevails through this trial, I will not." Lyla embraces me as I sob my fears into her shoulder. "I never thought it to be so, but I feel love for Turin and Jayx. But Zyvis? The idea of his touch fills me with such dread. I had hoped it to be different. I want to be with Turin and Jayx, but I know I cannot be with them unless I accept their brother."

Lady Lyla allows me to cry, holding me as my sister would.

"Damn his arrogance and temper," I say. "I was starting to feel strong again, to envision a future in which my sister and I would perhaps be reunited. Now I feel I will lose everything. I remove myself from Lyla's embrace and dry my eyes on my sleeves.

"This is not an easy path for a woman, Isla. One husband is an adjustment, but multiple mates? That's a challenge. I've learned from other Drakoryan brides that there is always one male who tests us more than the others."

"Turin said in the past the witches of the Mystic Mountain matched the woman to her dragon lords. The Lords of Za'vol chose me." I draw a ragged breath. "Oh, Lady Lyla... what if they chose wrong?"

She takes my face in her hands. "Then you will fight to make it right. You are a War Bride. You arrive at a time of conflict and even if the witches did not name you, I am convinced that fate still plays a role. The Lords of Za'vol need you. And you need them, even if you don't yet realize why or how."

"My Lady?" Sal appears at the door.

I rise, and she walks over and hands me a piece of parchment. I open it.

"It's Lord Turin," I say. "He wants a word with me before he goes to the council hall."

Lady Lyla smiles. "He likely wants to see if you are well since I stole you away. Let's find an attendant who can take you to him."

Nineteen

TURIN

The other lords are continuing to arrive as I send word to Isla. I should stay away, should start preparing for the council. I want to know that she is settled and well. I can't get the image of her curled on the floor from my mind.

I want to see her.

Just see her.

I tell myself that as I pace the hall of the bedchamber I've been given for my stay. Under normal circumstances, mated brothers stay away from their maiden until unmated ones have joined with her.

These are not normal circumstances.

There's a familiar catch in my throat when Isla walks through the door, and a familiar heat and hardness as my body responds to her very nearness. She is my true mate.

I try not to think of Zyvis. I experience a surge of jealousy each time I think of him lying with her, then a surge of fear over what will happen if he doesn't.

"You wanted to see me, my Lord Turin?"

"Yes." She looks up at me as I approach Her eyes are so green. I lift my hand to cradle the side of her face. "I wanted to see how you were faring."

She arches a brow. "My lord, I could have sent word by my maid if that's all you wanted to know."

I am not given to embarrassment, but I feel the heat of a flush creep up my neck. Isla sees it, too, and grins. She is so incredibly delectable. My gaze drops to the bodice of her gown. The tight swell of her nipples are visible through the fabric. She's looking up at me. Her lips are half-parted, and I can see the tip of her tongue.

Tradition be damned. I just want to hold her. That is all. I pull her to me and she allows it, her thin arms winding their way around my neck. I feel her soft sigh as I hear it. I bury my face in the waves of her hair. Her body is pressed against mine. I drop a hand to her lower back. I just want to touch her. That is all. I slide my hand down to cup her bottom. Just a squeeze and then I'll let her go. Her buttock is firm and springy in my grasp.

Just a taste. What can it hurt? My lips find hers. Isla moans against my mouth and I know I am lost to her. My hands are everywhere now, moving up to find an opening to her gown, but there is only a row of buttons along the back. She tears her mouth away from mine and presses it to my ear.

"Too many," she says. "And you cannot tear my gown." Her next words turn my cock to iron. "Lift my skirt and fuck me from behind." There's a plea in her words, desperate and wanton and vulnerable. I cannot spin her around fast enough. She bends over a nearby chair, grasping the arm. I lift her skirts, filled with appreciation at how the fabric frames the perfect globes of her ass. She looks back at me as she arches her back. I can see the fiery red fleece covering a labia parted to reveal deep pink inner petals. Her thighs are slick with a sheen of arousal, its presence revealing that she wanted this before she even entered my chamber. Her scent is intoxicating; I am as eager to have her as I was our first night together. I plunge two fingers into her pussy, coating them with her essence as I fist the length of my cock with my other hand. I withdraw my fingers and push my cock into her tight sheath; when she cries out, I lean forward and push my fingers into her mouth.

"Taste," I say. "It is your essence, and it is the nectar I long for every waking moment."

She closes her eyes and sucks my fingers as her pussy squeezes my cock with the same sweet rhythm. If the gods in their realms are the creators of bliss, then they have given me more than a measure.

I look down, admiring the spread halves of her bottom, mesmerized by the sight of my cock sliding in and out of her impossibly tight pussy. Her excitement has raised ridges along the length of my shaft. They pulse and move as I thrust in and out, stimulating her so thoroughly that she comes once, then twice.

Isla is careful not to scream, for what we do is secret. She leaves little marks on her balled fist where she bites down, but her body speaks for her. The rippling of her core grips and draws on my cock, and as much as I long to give her a third climax, she unmans me before I can. I feel my balls tighten to hard knots, feel the pressure of my seed surging, and am forced to brace myself with both arms to keep the weight of my upper body from falling on her.

It is the greatest feeling in the world, coming inside her, leaving her marked. As I reluctantly back away, I watch the pearlescent stream slide from the deep pink folds of her pussy. She is mine.

She is ours.

I step back. Did I imagine Jayx's voice in my head? I tuck my cock back under my skirt and lift Isla to standing. She turns to me and my heart aches to see how beautiful she is. Her eyes are half closed, her expression one of a satisfied woman.

"Isla of Branlock..."

"I know," she says, putting a hand to my face. I can still smell her scent on the fingers that graze my cheek. "I shall not tell."

She arranges her skirt. Despite my guilt, it pleases me to think that she will walk back to her chamber with my seed still seeping from her body.

"Girl!" I call to a castle maid as I walk Isla from the room. "Escort my lady back to the women's quarters."

Isla glances back as she leaves, her eyes brimming with love. I know she's thinking on what I called her. *My lady*. Real or imagined, Jayx's voice in my head reminds me of the truth. She is ours to share, and all depends now on the younger brother who must be made to understand the importance of control.

Twenty

JAYX

We gather in the throne room. To my left stands Turin, to my right Zyvis. I have cause to be annoyed with both. When I noted Turin's absence, I suspected he'd sought out Isla. It is difficult for a Drakoryan to close his mind in times of intense passion. I'd sought his and caught a glimpse of what he was feeling and thinking. I frown to think of it now. Our younger brother has not yet mated. Turin knows better. But there is no time to confront Turin, and even if I wanted to, to expose him in front of our hot-headed younger brother would only make thing worse than they are.

The creak of huge doors opening turns our collective attention towards the back of the throne room. Unlike other rooms of the castle, this one is austere by comparison. There is no adornment save for the Drakoryan banner on one wall and an ancient mural on another depicting a compendium of our history from the first Drakoryans created in the Mystic Mountain to the last battle of the ShadowFell.

Huge braziers blaze around a raised dais that holds five thrones — a higher one for the king with two on each side for the crown princes ,who remain silent during council. Their presence is a promise of continued rule. Everyone is deferential to the king.

King Vukurcis is coming. I see the top of his crown as he enters. The lords have turned in his direction, taking a knee as he passes. As those closest to me kneel, I get my first full glimpse of our liege, lowering my head in hopes that no one sees the shock I'm sure everyone else must be feeling.

Our king has aged. The gray hair is now white, and although his carriage is straight, and his stride is strong, this is a far different man than the one who successfully led us into battle.

Ahead of me, Drorgros of Fra'hir cuts his eyes in my direction as the king passes and I know this was unexpected for him, too. Like me, he is mindful of the contrast between King Vukurcis and the princes who retain the fullness of their prime. Like their father, the princes—Bymir, Rargi, Ygi, and Oneg—exude authority and power both in size and demeanor.

With most Drakoryan houses, when sons come of age, they leave their home for a new mountain. The name of that mountain becomes the name of their house. It is different for the King and his sons. There is no name for the King's Mountain. When a king dies, his sons battle for both the crown and a bride. The new king rules, with his brothers as advisors and sons born to him stay in his house. The sons of his brothers do not. They eventually leave for their own houses and become Lords who pass down their titles. It has been that way since the beginning of time. All Drakoryans can trace their lineage back to the original kings.

Each prince stands before his throne, but none sit until his father does. Once they do, all lords all rise in unison, and King Vukurcis speaks.

"Lords of the Empire..." His words resound through the hall with the shadow of a dragon's rumble. The voice of the king is distinct because it speaks to our dual natures like no other. "The old enemy has returned." He looks around the room, which is silent save for the crackling of the fire in the braziers. "We have defeated the ShadowFell in the past. Those wars were never easy. The one we face now will be the hardest of all."

"Our enemy has grown cunning. They hunger now for the humanity they sorely underestimated. The Mystic Mountain is now under constant guard for the there lies the magic they need to become half man. We have brought the villagers into the shadow of the empire for their own protection. Make no mistake. The enemy is watching. When it attacks, it will seek not only to become like us, but to displace us once and for all."

A chill falls over the room. The king is silent now. When he is silent, that means there is more.

"This is not the worst of it. By now, most of you know that there is a dark force compelling the ShadowFell to their nefarious ends. The Witches of the Wyrd do not yet know its name, but whatever god allies itself with the enemy is no friend of our creators. This god is just as as strong as ours, perhaps stronger. We need all our attention and effort fixed on victory."

The king's gaze falls on me and my brothers. Just as a house claims a mutual mate, so does it claim a mutual reputation. Zyvis has damaged ours.

"What we protect may also be our downfall if the villagers rise up and divide our attention against the enemy. Perhaps I erred in not holding this council before the decision was made to bring these humans under our protection. However, I did not think it necessary to remind trusted lords of the challenges this would bring, of the necessity of not increasing the natural resentment the ruled may feel for the rulers.

I cast a sidelong glance at Zyvis. His face is read with shame as the king continues.

"We have protected the villagers over the mountains, but we have also taken from them. We have claimed the fruits of their labor, stolen and mated and bred their daughters. If ever there was a time to combine restraint with authority, it is now.

Food will be moved from the Drakoryan castle storehouses to the village storehouse. It was Drakoryans who decided to wait before gathering the harvest and we must compensate the humans for our poor judgement. What was lost to them must be restored. The villagers must be allowed the same agency they enjoyed over the mountains. They must pick a leader from each village, a council, to represent them all. We will negotiate..."

"Negotiate? "Lord Udra's tone is incredulous. "We are their rulers!"

"We are." King Vukurcis fixes Lord Udra with a steely gaze. "And as rulers, we should recognize when to sacrifice pride for the greater good. We will need more than the villagers' obedience. We will need their patience during a winter that promises hunger and war.

"The king is right. We must regain the villagers' trust." The strong voice of another lord rises above the assembly. "But won't moving a portion of the food stores to the villagers' storehouse put it at risk should the ShadowFell attack the Empire? The food in the castle storehouses is hidden and guarded."

"And so it will be in the villages." King Vukurcis lifts a hand. "Where are the Lords of Kri'byl?

From across the aisle, five lords stand and move to approach the throne. The first two are identical in appearance. Tyri and Yrko of Kri'byl are twins, a rarity in the Drakoryan

Empire. They are both fierce warriors, with short-cropped hair and close-cropped beards. They share the same muscular build, and the same moon-shaped birthmark. On Lord Tyri, who was born first, the mark is on the left side of his chest. On Lord Yrko, on the right.

They are trailed by their three other brothers— Erdorin, Gryvrig, and Jareo. Beardless Erdorin wears his wavy hair at shoulder length. Gryvrig, with his russet hair and beard, stands out from his dark-haired brothers. Jareo wears his long hair in a single braid, and while he is beardless, a shadow of stubble gives his face a menacing appearance.

"Lords of Kri'byl." King Vukurcis leans forward. "You are tasked by your king with patrolling and protecting the village food stores. The villagers will see that we are as committed to the interests of all. You will be my ambassadors, ensuring villagers' loyalty to the empire while being the extension of my authority. You will keep the peace." He pauses. "You will do this by any means, but force will be the last resort."

"Lord Jayx of House Za'vol and Lord Tythos of House Fra'hir...you will take your best soldiers from those who humans who serve us now and go to the villagers. Our serving class is loyal. Perhaps they can help ease the fear and even recruit some new soldiers from the village. We need all – Drakoryans, our serving class, the villagers — to make defeating ShadowFell a common cause."

We speak more of war then, of strategy, of the need to patrol the borderlands between the empire and the mountains while protecting the villages, our castles, and the Mystic Mountain. King Vukurcis demands an accounting from each household's factor of food stores. We discuss the possibility of hunting for game beyond the mountains, or of taking villagers and servants to forage for wild mushrooms or tubers should the need arise. We must not underestimate the gnawing resentment that comes with gnawing hunger, the king tells us.

We speak of the witches, who have grown quiet in their mountains, who are wary to use their magic now lest the energy attract the ShadowFell. They hoard it now, in case of attack. Queen Arvika realizes the fate of the Drakoryans is tied to the fate of the coven under the mountain. When the time comes, the king tells us, dragons and witches and humans will fight together.

"War is coming." It is late in the day when the king rises. "After so many years on this throne, it's something you can feel, like a storm. The evil this one carries will test us all. It will mean the difference between our survival and our extinction." He pauses. "Tonight, we will hold what will be the last Drakoryan feast before the lean times begin. Return with your ladies. I would meet those I have not met. I could do with a bit of beauty." He smiles and then turns. "Go. Seek your rooms, except the Lords of Za'vol. I would have them remain for a word."

Twenty-One

ZYVIS

I keep my eyes averted as the other lords file from the throne room. I know the king is displeased with me. I know I have brought shame on my house.

"Lords of Za'vol." King Vukurcis' voice is weary. "I hope you will take heed of what I have said today about the need for restraint."

"We have, Your Highness," Jayx says. I can feel his gaze on me. I can feel Turin's.

Pride tightens its grip on my throat, whispering in my ear that I have nothing to explain, not even to the king. Pride sounds a lot like my father, but I fight it now and step forward.

"I take full responsibility," I say. "The villager challenged us."

The king leans back and strokes his long white beard. Beside him, the princes remain silent. I wish they were not here, watching their father demonstrate how to handle a rogue lord.

"I sense more to this situation." King Vukurcis is watching me thoughtfully. His focus shifts to my brothers. "I hear House Za'vol have taken a War Bride?"

"Yes," Turin says. "A maiden from Branlock."

"And you have all coupled with her?" The king arches a bushy brow, as if already knowing the answer.

"All save for me," I confide. "We gave the maiden time to adjust after coming to Castle Za'vol. Before I could take her, we were called here."

The king sighs. "While no excuse for threatening the villagers as you did, the heat of lust does make our dragon nature difficult to control." He nods to Jayx and Turin. "Your brother should have stayed behind to bed your bride while you went to the fields."

"We needed every available dragon," Jayx says.

"Hmmm." The king looks back at me. "Nothing can be done about the past. But you, Lord Zyvis, must go this moment and make that maiden yours. Slake your desire. Cool your blood that a cooler head may guide you through troubling times."

Relief washes through me. This is as close to royal forgiveness as I could hope for.

"Be gone now." He waves us off with a royal hand. "I will see you at the feast tonight, with a lady who has been fully claimed. Perhaps you can achieve the Deepening before you return to Castle Za'vol. You would be the first outside Drakoryan royalty to seal your bond within the walls of my castle."

We all bow gratefully. "Thank you, Your Majesty," Jayx says. "It would indeed be an honor."

As we leave the hall, I should be reflecting on the mercy of the king. He could have punished me for what I did; he could have punished our household. Instead, he has given me leave to claim Isla under his roof, and that is all I can focus on. My cock already stiffens under my leather skirt as I try to imagine the soft swells of her breasts, the taste of her arousal, the sounds she will make when I sink into her quivering warmth.

"Brother, a word?" Turin has stopped me with a hand on my arm.

"Make haste." I don't try to hide my impatience. "I'm on my way to Isla."

"That is why I want a word." Turin pulls me to the side. "Isla has been through great pain. The attack on her village affected her deeply."

"I am aware of this..." I snap. I try to pull my arm away, growing more annoyed when my brother tightens his grip. Jayx is at his side now.

"Isla seeks security. She will demand something of you before you couple..."

"Demand?" My father's voice interrupts us. We did not know he had been lurking nearby.

"Lord Urda, this is a private conversation," Jayx says.

My father's face turns red. "You forget yourself, young lord," he growls. "You had more than one father in the house that raised you up."

Turin releases his grip. "Yes." He faces my father. "But we have our own house now, and you have no place in our affairs unless asked."

"Bah!" My enraged father points his finger at me. "This is why you lost when you battled for your maiden, Zyvis. You allow your brothers to make you weak! Listen how they encourage you to allow a woman to make demands. A woman!" His eyes glow gold. The dragon in his veins is slow to wake, but it is stirring now, and despite the fact that I am younger and stronger, this is my father—the great Lord Udra — and I am afraid. He steps towards me, forcing me to look up at him. "Is this who you are?" he asks, disdain dripping from his voice. "Some simpering fool following your brothers' directions even in the bedchamber? Honor your father. Teach your woman that one Lord of Za'vol will not grovel before her like a dog."

Humiliation slices through me like the blade of a hot knife. I feel my jaw clench. He is right. Who are Jayx and Turin to tell me how to take this woman? I look to my brothers.

"I can handle Isla," I say. "Go prepare for the feast. If I need your advice, I'll ask you for it."

I do not look back as I storm away. If my brothers call, I do not hear them. I am fixed now on my need, on what I deserve. My father has refined my purpose, and he is right.

He is always right.

Twenty-Two

ISLA

I am practicing with my sword, trying to remember what Turin has taught me. I think of the sword as an extension of my arm. I move it fluidly. I seek to train my toughts as I train my movements. I only think fully on the ShadowFell when I am armed, when I can imagine killing the one that took my sister.

I imagine two stones of the fireplace to be dragon scales, the space between two of them the vulnerable spot where I must drive my sword. But as I draw back my arm, I hear the door open behind me. I turn, expecting to see Sal. When I spot Zyvis standing there, unannounced, I drop my arm to my side in surprise.

"Swordplay?" He closes the door behind him, gesturing to my wooden weapon as he approaches. He walks over and takes it from my hand studying it. "This belonged to my brother."

It occurs to me that I was practicing when Jayx first came

to me as well. This moment would feel familiar were it not for the disapproving look on Zyvis' face.

"Yes," I say. "Turin gave it to me."

"The sharpest thing a lady should wield is a tapestry needle."

When I try to take hold of the sword, Zyvis holds it aloft. I feel like a child reaching for a toy. It makes me angry, and the helpless feeling I've been fighting replaces the bravery I've been trying to grow.

It occurs to me then that he does not understand. Perhaps if I explain. I lower my hand. "Did your brothers not tell you?" I ask.

"Tell me what?" Zyvis walks over and puts the sword on a shelf far too high for me to reach. I try to quell the anger rising along with the growing helplessness.

"What I would have from you before we couple," I say. "That is why you are here, isn't it?"

Zyvis turns back to me. There is no understanding in his tone, only mockery. "What you would *have* from me? Are you a village whore that you demand payment?"

I feel as if the wind has been knocked out of me. "No!" The word is forced out by an exasperated breath. "But if I am to go willingly to your bed..."

Zyvis walks over to me. "Enough!" He's a hands-width away from me, glaring in the room's warm light. "Were it not for the Drakoryans, you'd be dead at the bottom of a well instead of warm in the castle of a king."

"Were it not for the Drakoryans, the ShadowFell would have seen no need to attack my village." I pause. "I am no whore, Lord Zyvis." I glare up at him. "Apologize."

The muscle of his jaw clenches. Although my heart is pounding, I do not look away.

"I apologize for offending you," he says. "However, I will promise you nothing. You either lie with me or you don't."

Oh, how I want to refuse. He is unlike his brothers, and the memory of their sweetness, so easily juxtaposed to his arrogance, makes me want to turn away. Only love for Jayx and Turin, for what they will lose – for what I will lose— if I do not lie with Zyvis, forces me to drop my gaze.

"Very well, Lord Zyvis. I will lie with you." I search his face for signs of disappointment, given the flatness of my tone. Instead, I see only selfish lust.

He takes me by the upper arms and pulls me to him. I had taken a rest earlier, and before I did, Sal had helped me change into a light shift. I'd given her leave afterwards. Now I wish I'd asked her to stay.

Zyvis reaches for the neck of my garment. I close my eyes as the fabric rips and he pushes the torn garment roughly from my body. Even though we aren't touching, I can feel the heat emanating from his bare chest. I can feel his hungry gaze on my nakedness. His hand closes over my right breast. His stern look dares me to challenge the authority in his touch.

"I will make you scream with pleasure." It is a boast delivered with gruff certainty, but also a detachment, as if this is something Zyvis is determined to do to prove he can.

I do not reply and when he kneels to the floor and lays me on the rug by the fire, I stare up at the candles on the wall sconces, at the tongues of flame that dance as Zyvis' tongue begins to dance between my legs.

He is tasting me as if I were ripe fruit, lapping and stabbing. I bite my lip, seeking to deny him the dual responses of shock and arousal that overwhelm me. I feel my hips rise towards his mouth. I dig my fingers into the fur of the rug under me, twisting hands full of it as his possessive touch roams rough over my body. I whimper in frustration as my nipples harden under his palms. I do not want to surrender to him, and to my relief he stops before I reach pleasure's peak.

Zyvis is on his knees now, pulling me to mine.

"Did my brothers teach you how to please a man with your mouth?" he asks.

I shake my head and he grins wolfishly.

"Of course, they didn't." He pushes my head down, towards his exposed cock. It is long and thick and bulges like a muscle. The end is flared, like a fleshy arrow. He drives my head towards it and I know what he wants. Men use their tongues and fingers to penetrate and tease. I can use my mouth as I use my pussy, can use the warmth and heat, can use my tongue as they use theirs.

I remember what Lady Klea said, about how a woman's submission can be her weapon. I will use mine and make him weak. I lean down, laving Zyvis with my tongue. I move my mouth across the flared head of his cock. He groans. I slide it down. He is so large that I don't get far so I nurse the end of his cock like a babe. He goes rigid. His balls tighten where I hold them. I back off, denying him his climax. I fist the base of his shaft, running my hand up, noting where my touch makes him groan the loudest. He thinks I am serving him, but I am not. I am learning to control him. I flick my tongue against the spot at the base of his head where a translucent drop appears from the slit. I flick it away. He grabs my hair. He is impossibly hard. I put my hand on his chest and lean over him.

"Oh, my Lord Zyvis," I say throatily. I look up at him. His grin is satisfied, swayed by my submissive tone. Without warning, I throw my leg over him, sinking down onto his shaft. He is so large that I gasp. The youngest Lord of Za'vol is as unprepared for my pussy as I was for his tongue, and just as helpless. I tighten my muscles against him as I lean over, my breasts dangling like ripe fruit just out of his reach. They bob and sway as I rise and lower myself once, twice.

The look on his face is one of surprise, his sudden spurt of hot seed my victory. I do not reach climax as I force his. He grasps my hips, writhing beneath me, trapped between my soft white thighs as I stare down at him. When I have wrung the last of his tribute from his cock, I rise to standing.

"Congratulations on claiming me, Lord Zyvis," I say.

I turn away then, tears stinging my eyes. I have given myself to a man I do not love for the sake of two I do. Still, it is a hollow victory, and not just for me. I brace myself for his anger, but a moment later I hear the door shut as Zyvis leaves the room.

Twenty-Three

JAYX

I want to ask her if she is all right. I want to ask if Zyvis treated her gently.

We are in the hallway outside the Queen's quarters, where we all waited for Isla to emerge. It has been hours since our brother left to be with her, and although we did not discuss it, I know Turin has been worried, too.

It is hard to be angry with the king, but I was unsettled when he granted Zyvis permission to go to Isla. I imagine her, unprepared for a mate fueled by the meanness of his father. I feel a flush of anger when I think of Lord Udra's interference.

I do not know what happened between Zyvis and Isla. I only know that he is uncharacteristically quiet. I'd like to think it is from relief that comes with the unleashing of lust, but when Isla arrives, they exchange only brief glances before she turns her attention to me and Jayx. She smiles, and I forget my worries.

"Are you well, my lady?" I ask.

"I am yours," she says, giving me her small hand. The other she rubs down Jayx's arms. He smiles, too, and we admire her beauty. She is resplendent in a gown of sage-colored brocade covered in delicately embroidered vines flowering with tiny plum-colored flowers. The split gown reveals an underskirt of the same color as the blooms. The neckline of the gown dips low. A single tear-drop shaped green amethyst hangs just above the dip of her cleavage. Her hair is swept into a thick coil of braids that wraps around the top of her head to converge in a long thick plait in the back.

All lords believe their lady is the finest in the Drakoryan Empire, but tonight even King Vukurcis seems impressed when it is our turn to approach the dais just prior to the feast. It is said the king has always had an eye for exceptional beauty, and his lingers on Isla as she curtsies before the throne.

"The War Bride of House Za'vol," he says. "And a brighter flame never burned in my hall than you." He laughs then, looking left and right to the princes. "When it comes time to take a bride, you should do so well." Beside me, Isla blushes beautifully, and the king chuckles.

"I take it that the final bond will also take place here?"

"Yes, Your Majesty," I answer for all of us.

The king smiles. "My oracle will guide the way. Again, it will be my honor, and I will consider a newly completed union to be a positive omen as we prepare for victory over the ShadowFell."

His words are more optimistic than they were in the throne room, and I'm sure this is because our ladies are in attendance and he would soothe their fears on what will likely be our last happy night before the war.

I try to concentrate on this night as we head to the feast. This is our night, the night we finally achieve the Deepening. When we return to Castle Za'vol, we will be a bonded family ready to face an uncertain future together.

The last feast before war. It is only fitting that this, too, should be at the king's castle. Dragons are fabled for their appetites. Drakoryan appetites exceed those of humans in all things, be it food or sex. Our feast honors our love of good food, and a king's table offers the finest. The feast hall is the largest room in the castle. Banners representing each Drakoryan houseline one long wall. A single fireplace stretches the length of the other, huge logs blazing within.

And then there are the tables. They stretch nearly as far as we can see. I look down at Isla, who stares wide-eyed at the array of food. Whole roasted steers, pigs, and lambs sit steaming on massive platters. In between are the fowl — roast geese filled with a stuffing made from berries and grains, peafowl ringed by a circle of orange-glazed quail, pheasants baked in sage honey.

I laugh when Isla scowls at a tureen filled with stewed eels, and tell her there is something for all tastes, from the fish and mussel stew to venison pies to rabbit in gravy. Would she prefer trout? I ask this as we take our seats, eager to see her fed. She has been quiet since she appeared from her chamber. I want to attribute it to fatigue both from travel and Zyvis' attention. Perhaps some chestnut soup? Turin offers this, and I look over to see if Zyvis is offering her anything. His attention is focused on his father, who sits farther down the table, frowning as we dote on our bride. A passing maid carries a jug of wine, and although Isla's goblet is within reach, Zyvis holds out his own. Across the table, Lord Udra smirks in satisfaction. I think of his fatherly advice. I think of Isla's expectations. I try not to be angry. The mating is done. The time for anger is past. Once we achieve the Deepening and bond, Zyvis will appreciate her more. He will see the error of his ways.

"Chestnut soup." Turin holds a spoon to our mate's mouth. She sips the offering and smiles. A drop remains on her top lip. I pick up a napkin to blot it away and find myself putting my mouth to hers instead, tasting the soup, tasting her. Isla smiles at me, but there is something sad in her eyes.

She is tired. She is still adjusting. All will be well.

Try the pigeon pie. Try the oxtail soup. Try the honeyed figs. We ply her with food as we eat our own. Farther down the table, they are singing songs of war. The king's voice booms above the rest. He is rallying us, stoking the Drakoryan brotherhood. Soon, we are singing, too—ancient songs from battles of old, of heroes who fought the men who saw us as abominations, driving some to the other side of the world and subjugating others to grow our food and mates. I reach for a prawn the size of my fist as a bard begins reciting a poem recounting our conquering of the mountain people who now serve in our households and armies. It reminds us of that humans can be loyal, and provides hope that the villagers will be loyal, too.

Isla is nibbling on a candied fig as we ply her with more treats. We feast on a bit of everything, swallowing gulps of meat in between bites of brown bread flavored with olives. Our plates empty as hers piles higher with food we want her to try — fig tarts, marzipan, candied ginger, poached pears, cream puddings. She nibbles, but not enough to suit me.

It will be different when we get home, I tell myself. Even if there is rationing, even if we have to go without, Isla will have the best we can give her. She will feel love every moment.

I'm sure it seems impossible to her that every bite of the feast laid out on the king's table is consumed within hours. But for me, what awaits is more satisfying, and when we are summoned to the castle oracle's tower, I allow optimism to rise in me like the headiness of a rich wine.

* * *

Ezador the Wise is the oldest being in the Empire. He has served every king from the beginning, his unnatural long life granted to him by the witches who use him not only as their most powerful conduit but also as the keeper of Drakoryan history. He is the author of the books on both Drakoryan and ShadowFell history that grace every castle library in the empire. In a room below his, castle scribes spend long days hunched over parchment, recording the oracle's musings, formulas, and observations.

I tell Isla about him as we rise through the upper level of the castle in a special iron lift operated by dozens of male servants turning a circular crank below.

"He must be very stooped and aged by now," she says, and for the first time, Zyvis speaks up.

"You'll be surprised. Ezador may be wise, but he's also vain. He uses a glamour."

"A glamour?" It's clear she's never heard the term, but there's no time for an explanation. The lift stops at an arched wooden doorway with ornate iron hinges. When Jayx raps on it, a quiet voice orders us to enter.

Twenty-Four

ISLA

This is no wizened old man. An ethereally youthful face stares out at us from beneath the hood of a purple robe marked with glowing symbols that change and move in the dim light of a room that is part library, part apothecary, part collection of oddities. While my mates have assured me that Ezador's study is typical of oracles, the man himself is anything but what I imagined.

He is so radiantly beautiful that it's difficult to discern his gender. His features are soft and gentle, his skin flawlessly smooth, his eyes an enchanting silver gray. I understand now; a glamour is some kind of magic used to alter his appearance.

The oracle's eyes are fixed on me. He walks over to study me. He reaches out a hand, brushing it lightly over my hair. I feel as if I'm being read like a book. Even his voice is beautiful —soft and silky smooth, but with an air of quiet authority.

"Oh, if only I preferred the company of females over males. You would almost do." He grins and winks at my mates. "Even if I did, you have three dragon lords to protect your favors."

His tone is teasing. I stare at him. I've never met anyone like this oracle, who turns away and walks to the center of the room. There is a strange circle drawn on the floor. Around it are symbols similar to the ones on his robe. In the center of the circle is a chair.

"Are you ready for the final step in your journey? Are you ready to leave Isla of Branlock in your past and become Lady Isla of Za'vol?"

"Good sir," I say. "I will always be Isla of Branlock."

He smiles serenely. "Ah, so you will. You are a War Bride. You have a War Bride's fighting spirit." He pauses. "You are not the first, you know, but you are the first War Bride of this age. It is a rare thing." He gestures for me to approach, and when I do, he orders me to hold out my hands. When I obey, he places his palm down on mine.

"These hands..." His eyes meet mine. "They long to hold a sword. To strike and kill. You seek a reckoning."

"A dragon slaughtered my village. It took my sister."

He closes his eyes. When he opens them, the pupils are gone, replaced by a silver haze and the voice that comes from his mouth is female.

"Two dragons threaten your future. One you will help defeat, the other you will defeat alone."

"What do you mean?" I ask, but the oracle does not answer.

"He likely does not know." Turin's voice behind me is quiet. He and his brothers still stand outside the circle. "This message comes from the Mystic Mountain, from the Witches of the Wyrd."

Ezador's eyes clear and he gestures again, with flourish, to the chair. When I take a seat, he motions for the Lords of

Za'vol to approach. They lay hands on me as he retrieves a book bound in dragon scale.

Ezador stands before us. "Close your eyes, pretty child," he says. I do, and hear his voice chanting in a strange, guttural tongue. It is words, but not words. I know this is the language of dragons. I feel as if I'm sinking into softness, and my eyes open. But not *my* eyes. I'm looking through someone else's eyes and feel a pressure on my toes that makes me giggle from deep in my belly. I look down. It's Lady Klea, younger, and smiling. She's playing with my toes.

"Such tiny feet, Lord Jayx," she says. "You'd better be careful, or mama will gobble them up!" She pretends to eat my toes and I raise my tiny fists towards her, reaching for her unbound hair. I feel such love, such safety where I lay in the comfort of my cradle, under my mother's loving gaze. She moves from my line of sight and I begin to wail as I turn my head to look for her, but I only see the window and the light from it grows brighter as I dissolve and am pulled towards it. I am spinning through the glare, and when I land, I am looking down at legs.

Dragon legs.

Razor sharp talons extend from the ends of huge, scaly feet. I feel clumsy, disoriented. It is my first time in dragon form, and the pain of shifting is seeping out of my body to be placed by wonder. I lean forward and instinctively catch myself with the joint of my wing, which functions as an extra limb to help me walk.

"Good! Good!" My father, Lord Orys, is below me. I arch my neck, surprised to see him so small when I have always looked up to him. "Look at yourself, Jayx. Don't be afraid! Go on!"

There is a pool to my left. I catch my reflection. It is fearsome. My skin is nubby and thick. Horns rise from my head, and around it, thick and flexible dragon spines. My father shouts directions, telling me how to move. Ahead of me is a ridge.

"Fly!" he tells me. "Fly! You were made for it, my son! Fly!"

I propel myself forward with my sturdy limbs. Then I straighten myself and extend my wings, taking two thunderous steps before rising through the air. It is natural, but it is terrifying. I have just leapt from one of the highest ledges in the kingdom. Wispy clouds float below me. I dive and fully spread my leathery wings for the first time, catching an air current and riding it upward. I turn my face towards the sun. A roar fills the sky. It is mine. I have found my dragon voice.

Suddenly, I'm falling, and everything is dark. War. We are at war. I smell fire and blood. The soldiers had aimed the huge harpoon at my enemy, at the black dragon. I'd seen them do it, but something has gone terribly wrong. I emerge from a rising plume of smoke to see the spear coming towards me. Pain rips through my body, pain like nothing I've never known. I feel blood pouring from my chest as the wind rushes past me. I hit the ground with such force that all goes black.

It is light again. My father and I stand on a balcony, looking out at the empire. The sun is rising. My father tells me peace is once again upon the land. He is proud of me. I have both served and led well as a Drakoryan knight in the king's army. We can hope again, and his hope is for the sons of his house to have happiness. There is one more fleeting memory, of a face. My face. I am looking at myself through Jayx's eyes. I am happier than I have ever been.

All goes dark once more, then clears like the sky after a storm.

Turin. I am Turin. I know because my mother is calling my name, telling me to be careful, to leave this task to someone else. I call back, telling her not to worry. There is no one else, and if I do not help, the lamb will die.

We'd been walking together when we'd heard it bleating. I'd rushed to the edge of the grassy ridge we were traversing and had seen it—a lamb that had toppled from the edge to land on a little jut of rock. It was frozen in fear. Large eagles swooped nearby, waiting for it to take a step so they could snatch it away. I could hear its mother calling for it as I ignored my own mother's warning and scurried downward, picking my way over the rocks. Below me, the river rolled. It had been a rainy spring and the water level was high. The sound of the rushing water roared in my head. I ignored it. I ignored my mother. I could not bear to think of the little creature, so frightened, so alone.

I am strong, even for a lad of nine summers. I lay down flat on a sun-warmed stone and stretch. My arms are just long enough to grasp the lamb by the ear. It cries out in pain as I snatch it up, continuing to struggle as I right myself. It takes balance and control to throw it over my shoulders, but I do, grasping its fore and hind legs in front of me as I use my free hand and legs to scale the rocks. At the top of the ridge, I find my mother half mad from worry and fear. Then her face softens as she sees the reunion between the ewe and lamb.

"That was not wise, Turin." Her relieved face is level with mine. I am as tall as she is now.

"No." I hug her. "But it was the right thing to do."

"Turin the savior." Lady Klea beams with pride as I look at her through the eyes of the man who will one day save me from the well. Then she recedes from view.

I am a dragon. I am above the clouds, a puffy blanket of white with gaps like holes revealing the earth below one. The sun flashes off the orange of my wings. I revel in the wind on my face. I inhale the scents of the earth below. I am slowing, drifting to where the clouds are thinner. There is a village below. I rise back above the clouds, which are thinning. I peer through the mist, my dragon sight allowing me to see the village that cannot see me.

It is Branlock. It is all here, from the village well to the cottages to the little stream where my sister and I washed our clothes. To Turin, this is but a simple memory of a routine patrol. Still, to me, it is a treasure, because I can revisit it whenever I want through his eyes. It will allow me to remember what it looked like before, allow me to remember that it existed. Thanks to Turin, I will never forget my home. My heart swells with gratitude and love. These memories are more than insights; they are gifts.

And now it is time for the final memories, those of Zyvis. I am staring into a black mist. It clears, and I see Lord Udra. He is looking at a round target with a knife stuck in the center. He smiles. "Well done, my son. You have fine aim. I am proud."

Something is wrong, though. This doesn't feel like the other memories. It is the difference between having an experience and looking at a picture. I feel nothing, and the image dims and fades like smoke. It is rapidly replaced with other images— all fleeting recollections that I cannot quite fathom or grasp before they disappear.

What is happening? I try to ask but cannot speak. The three sets of hands are still on me, yet one pair is shaking and sweating, as if the owner is under great strain.

Another image. I am in battle. I am a violet dragon filled with rage. I fight for the woman on the wall. I want to win her. I must. This, I finally feel. I strike my brothers with tooth and claw. I burn them with fire. They flee. I am victorious. Then the image shatters like glass— shatters because it is not real. I emerge from my trance to realize Zyvis was not giving me true memories, but ones he wished he could give me. Even after he removes his hands, I feel his shame clinging where his palms had been.

I open my eyes. The room is quiet.

"It failed. The bond was not made." The oracle's delivers the words with puzzled sympathy.

I feel a lump rise in my throat. "We are not mates, then?"

"It is all or none, child. One did not give what was needed for the true bond."

"Zyvis..." Jayx hisses. "Is this your revenge for not getting first rights? To deny us all..."

"No." I stand and face the two men I love in defense of the one I do not. I look to Zyvis, whose face has grown pale. "I do not think he wanted this outcome any more than you did, than I did."

My eyes meet Zyvis' and in them I see the shame I felt in his touch, the hurt. It is like a wall between us. I turn to the oracle.

"Is that it then? Are we to be..." I can barely say the word. "Apart?"

"You are a War Bride, child, remember? It depends on how hard you and those you love are willing to fight."

Twenty-Five

TURIN

In a Drakoryan household, we try to lift one another up, to complement and strengthen one another. It is hard now, and as we embark for home I cannot help but think of our own upbringing, of the discord in the household that raised us.

My parents tried to hide it, and as youthful lads are wont to do, we were too distracted to allow ourselves to notice. But there was strife, and I wish now that my parents had been more open about how my father and Jayx's handled Lord Udra.

A failure for one is a failure for all.

The trip home was especially somber. The one thing we'd hope to have — a secured mating— still eludes us. Time was against us. In addition to the worry of war, a single thought plagued us: If Zyvis could not achieve a Deepening with Isla, our own bond would be useless. She will have to leave the castle.

"Spar with me."

I've come to visit her when she makes the request. It's five days since we returned. Tension hangs over the empire like a haze, despite the Drakoryans' haste to fill the villagers' storehouse. None of us has touched Isla. Zyvis avoids her from shame of having failed to bond. Jayx and I are mindful that we cannot treat her as a full mate now that the Deepening has failed. Still, I long to be near her, to please her. In the evenings, I come to teach her swordplay. And this time I have a surprise.

"You can no longer spar with that." I point at the little wooden sword I'd given her.

"You think I'm not good enough with it?" Her umbrage makes me smile.

"No. I think you're too good. I think it's time to move beyond a wooden sword." I've had my hand behind my back and I move it now, to offer her a new gift — a sword forged especially for her.

Isla is speechless. She lays the wooden sword gently on the table and approaches me, reaching out to run her fingers along the leather scabbard that holds her new weapon. Her touch is reverent.

"For me? Truly?" The look of gratitude in her beautiful green eyes makes my heart lurch with love.

"Truly." I pause. "Things are..." I struggle to find the words. "Things are not as I thought they would be for us. I do not know what will happen. I do not know..." I feel a lump in my throat. I have not shed a tear since I was a child, but I am close now. I clear my throat. "I never want you to forget what we had, should we have to part."

Tears glitter in her eyes. She takes my gift and nods. "Thank you, my lord. I still keep faith. I've come this far."

"Yes, you have." I force a smile and then nod down at the sword. "In the days of men, knights of old named their swords, believing names gave them power. Will you name yours?"

Isla takes the sword and unsheathes it. The blade glimmers in the light. "I shall call it Fell Slayer, for it shall kill the dragon that burned my village." The look in her eyes is fierce. I cannot help marvel at her certainty.

"Fell Slayer." I take the scabbard from her and fasten its strap about her waist, before stepping back. "Let us see you wield it. The balance is different than your wooden one."

I draw my blade. Isla does the same. She extends Fell Slayer and smiles. "It feels good."

"This one is lethal, lady. Be careful that I am not the first dragon you slay."

She grins, but the fierceness is still in her eyes. It always is when we spar. She obeys my instructions. I tell her to follow the sword as much as she wields it, to think of it as the point of her finger as she jabs and slices. Drakorayns learn the art of wielding weapons of men, even though our mightiest strength is in our dragon nature. My brothers and I have trained both our fellow Drakoryan lords and human soldiers in combat. Isla is a natural, with instincts that surprise me. While she may lack the strength of a man, she compensates with a catlike quickness. Her movements tell me she spends her solitary hours practicing.

I end the lesson before she is ready. I always do. "I wish I could tarry longer, but I must away to the village."

Isla sheathes her sword. "Take me with you?"

I hate to refuse her, but I must. "Isla, the village is no place for a lady."

"You keep calling me that, yet I am not yet a lady."

"Isla..."

"I'm *not*." She sighs. "So much is fractured. My life. Your life. The bond between you and Jayx and Zyvis. I feel I am the cause of the latter."

I tilt her chin up so that she's looking into my eyes. "You are *not* the cause of this strife. Your arrival only illuminated what we have denied." I shake my head. "Or what our family has denied, even my parents. Zyvis' father..." My words trail off. I do not need to concern Isla with matters that are not of her concern.

"Lord Udra. Yes." She nods, understanding. "He is unpleasant, and Zyvis is afraid of him."

"How do you know this?"

"At the Deepening, the thoughts he shared were not real. He made them up. I am sure of it. He wanted me to see a son who was loved by his father. The last memory he shared was of something that did not happen. So they were all false." A look of sadness clouds her pretty features. "Where is Zyvis? I thought he would come to me, to try and fix what is broken."

I loathe to tell her the truth, but I cannot lie. "Awaiting the arrival of the last person he needs to see now. His father is coming."

"Lord Udra? Why?"

"Because he will never stop trying to control Zyvis. And only the direct son of a lord can turn him away from his door. Zyvis is not strong enough." I turn away. "I'm away to the village now."

"Take me with you." She's not dropping this. Isla moves in front of me, blocking my path. "I am a village girl. What better person to convince the villagers that it is not the Drakoryans who should be feared? I have seen the enemy. I have felt his awful fire." Isla takes my hand. "Please."

Normally this is a decision requiring the consultation of my brothers. But Isla is right. She is not yet our lady, not with the Deepening having failed.

"Very well," I say. "But I want you to stick close to me, understand?"

She arches a brow. "Of course. I have you for protection." Her hand drops to the hilt of Fell Slayer. "And my sword."

Twenty-Six

JAYX

Releg of Darly has not forgotten the slight he suffered. He has not forgotten the Drakoryan lord who loomed over him in dragon form.

I'm sitting by a newly dug well with the five Lords of Kri'byl. We have laid nearly all the rock about the well's mouth, and now village men are erecting the wooden frame that will hold the rope and bucket for drawing water. Releg is one of those men, and despite having faced a dragon, defiance remains in his eyes.

The lords of Kri'byl are unmated. Perhaps this is why the king has them making a home among the villagers. Still, it is not an easy assignment. The five have had to leave the comforts of their castle in the southern portion of the valley to live rough in the settlement. I know the goal is to build loyalty, but it is not a coveted task for any Drakoryan.

As we share a cup of water, a woman is approaching. We exchange surprised looks when she calls to us.

"Dragon lords!" We stand as she approaches. She wears the simple dress of a villager – dark brown overdress over a white chemise. And while the other women wears brown cloaks, hers is the green cloak of a healer. "I am in need of herbs and roots—milk thistle, nettle, burdock, and others."

"Do you need a guide to take you gathering?" Tyri, the eldest son of Kri'byl is first to address the woman.

"I need no guide," she snaps. "I know the places where these herbs should grow. I find none, not even beyond the marsh."

Tyri's twin, Yrko speaks up now. "The villagers have been ordered to stay within the boundaries. Permission is required to go to the marsh."

"I have never sought permission to acquire what I need to heal." She glares from beneath her cloak. "I will not seek it now."

A muscle twitches in Yrko's cheek. "I am not scolding you..."

"I don't care if you are." This woman only comes up to our chests, but she is challenging us all as she looks from one face to the other. "I have a mother who is about to give birth, and others soon to deliver after her. I do not have the herbs I need. Unless I miss my guess, you all have castle apothecaries. You will bring me what I need."

"You are commanding for one so small." Erdorin, another brother, speaks up. "And disrespectful."

"Will you turn into a dragon to frighten me, big man?" She smirks. "Before you do, you should know I won't cower like my uncle."

So, she is kin to Releg. This explains much.

Her words drip with scorn and defiance as she continues. "If it will help sway you, the woman who needs my help has already birthed three daughters, each more beautiful than the last. I'm sure this babe will be a daughter, too. Would you risk her losing the child if it means one less future maiden for your kind to steal away?"

I look to the Lords of Kri'byl; this healer is clearly trying their patience. When Erdorin steps towards her, she holds her ground.

"What is your name?" he demands to know.

"Thera, not that my name matters."

Erdorin regards her in silence before turning to me. "Lord Jayx, would you arrange to have Thera the Healer supplied with what she needs?"

I nod. "I will ask our oracle. If we do not have all she requires, the oracle who serves Castle Jo'lyn dabbles in all manner of herbs. No doubt we can stock her shelves."

Thera inclines her head towards the left. "My cottage is not yet built. There are others more in need, so I am making do in a tent on the outskirts of the village. Healers live apart from others. I will need the herbs brought there." She turns on her heel without another word and walks away.

"A sharp tongue wags in that pretty mouth," Jareo says. The youngest lord of Kri'byl is scowling in the direction of the healer as she disappears from view. He looks to the rest of us. "In the past, her entire village would have paid for her rudeness. We'd have burned their land."

"We are no longer in the past," Gryvrig, the second-born says. "Any land we burn now is our own."

"There should be consequences, just the same," Jareo insists.

"She's a woman." Erdorin waves his hand dismissively. "It will avail us nothing to dignify her impertinence. Her defiance is as significant as an ant's."

"Don't be so sure." I weigh in now. As small as the healer is, her eyes burn with a fire I've seen before. She reminds me of Isla. "It is unwise to discount the determination and strength of female will. They have a power of their own."

"Only when we take them as mates," Gryvrig counters. "We rely on them for our bloodline. But a healer? She will not be given leave to speak to us like that again."

The five move back towards the well, their time for rest over. I turn my attention to calling Turin, using my mental connection to tell him herbs are needed. I know he is coming to the village. I want to make sure the healer is satisfied. Regardless of what the Lords of Kry'bril say, I sense Thera of Darly is not to be underestimated.

Twenty-Seven

ISLA

We'd been about to leave the castle when Turin had gotten a message from Jayx about the healer's needs. The oracle of Castle Za'vol is as different from the king's oracle as night is from day. Plump and taciturn, Ovir the Wise is slovenly by comparison, the hem of his brown robes tattered from dragging on the flagstones. He grumbles as he fills a basket with the herbs the healer requested, then grumbles again when I request more. I ignore him. I want to bring more than has been requested, so I add things the women in Branlock used—crampbark and chamomile and mint.

"She's not the only healer," I tell Turin as we leave. "Each village had one. We will need to make sure they are all supplied, at least until we can grow or gather more herbs."

"Worry not," he tells me as he puts me up on a horse. It's my first time riding since I left Branlock. My gray mare fidgets as he climbs on his larger horse.

"I want to take the herbs to the healer." I shift in my

saddle, feeling the sheathed sword at my waist move against my leg.

"As you wish." Turin clicks his tongue and his horse moves off. Mine follows, picking up a bouncy trot. In the distance, I can see the Mountain of Kings and beside it the Mystic Mountain, dragons wheeling around or perched on its peak. King Vukurcis has increased the protection of the sacred home of the witches, and Turin tells me that five Drakoryan lords also stay in the villages, ready and able to transform and protect should the need arise.

The horses cover the ground at a speedy trot as clouds gather overhead. By the time we arrive on the outskirts of the settlement, something wet and cold falls on my face. Snow, light and persistent. The growing village teems with activity, even though it is bitter cold and late in the day. The rate of expansion is impressive, a testament to the village will that I remember all too well.

My horse follows Jayx towards a tent apart from the construction. It is round and covered with skins tied to pegs in the ground. Smoke rises from the top, and as we approach, my mare startles at the sound of a blood-curdling scream.

I am nearly unseated by my spooking horse, which would have bolted had Jayx not grabbed the reins.

"Are you all right?"

"Yes," I say, shaking slightly. I climb down from my mount, happy to be off as I take the basket. From the tent, another scream can be heard. Even if my horse is startled, I am not. I recognize the sounds of a woman giving birth. I tell Turin I should go alone. When I tell him why, he agrees. Men want no part of birthing. It scares them, even men who are half dragon. He tells me to stay put, that he will come back for me. As he leads my horse away, I turn and walk into the tent.

Although I know the sounds of birth, I have never witnessed one. When I enter the tent, I see a woman lying by the fire. She is older than both me and the woman who kneels between her legs. The healer's sharp-featured face is rapt in concentration as she presses down on what looks like a blood-covered, hairy ball emerging from between the laboring mother's legs.

"Breathe, Ela. You can do this. Breathe the babe out."

The healer glances up at me, then looks away, deferring her curiosity as she returns her focus on the baby she's delivering.

"Aaaaaaagggggghhhhh!" The laboring mother's renewed wail fills the tent.

"Ela!" The healer calls her name in a commanding voice. "Breathe it *out*. You've done this before. You will do it again."

The mother lays her head down and shuts her eyes. She emits a guttural, breathy groan and pushes. The baby's head emerges between her legs, its features compressed into a scowl.

"Good. Good!" The healer cradles the head, swooping her finger into the infant's mouth. The babe, its body still inside its mother, emits a tiny cough.

"Once more," the healer demands, and the laboring woman complies, her huge egg of a belly deflating as the infant slips from her amid a rush of clear fluid. The healer catches the infant, which spreads its arms and legs wide. The babe is still scowling, its eyes scrunched tight in its pink face. I watch, fascinated, as the healer flips the infant over and unwraps a thick purple cord looped around its body. When she turns the baby back up, a lusty scream resounds through the tent. The smile on the exhausted mother's face is both relieved and sad. I know what she must be thinking. Months ago, she'd expected her baby to be born in her own village, in a cottage that would see it warm and well-fed through the winter, not here, not into this uncertainty.

"Take your daughter." The healer puts the newborn on her mother's chest. The cord that connected them pulses more slowly with each passing second. As mother coos at her babe, it turns its ruddy face to the sound of her voice, its expression curious and alert. The healer stands, glances at me, and walks to a basin, where she washes her hands before returning to cover the new mother with a blanket.

"I've come with herbs," I tell her. "One of the Drakoryan sent me."

"A woman with a sword and a fine dress." She walks over and takes the basket, ignoring me as she begins to inspect the contents. "What village are you from that they dress so?"

"Branlock," I say.

She looks up at me curiously. "Branlock? Branlock was burnt. The maidens all taken."

"All but me. I alone survived. In a well." I pause. "I am Isla."

"I am Thera, Healer of Darly." She takes the basket to the fire, where she begins to mix one of the herbs with water in a little cauldron hanging above the flame. As the contents start to cook, she peers at me through the steam. "What village has taken you in now that Branlock is no more?"

"None." Outside the wind howls and I wait for it to settle before continuing. "Three Drakoryans saved me and took me for a mate. A War Bride, they call me."

She smirks. "Well, that explains the fine dress. Tell me, Isla of Branlock. Will you sleep well in your castle, knowing that the rest of us are trapped in a conflict between dragons?"

The harshness of her question takes me aback. "I did not choose my fate any more than a maiden snatched from a rock." My voice is shaking with anger. "Who are you to judge?"

Thera the healer doesn't immediately reply. Instead, she ladles tea into a wooden cup, which she blows across to cool. "Drink, Ela," she says, pressing the cup to the woman's lips. "It will help you expel the afterbirth. I've mixed in something to ease the pain."

Only after Ela has downed the tea does the healer return to where I stand.

"I don't judge you. I do judge what men who become dragons make us become—docile brides, beaten men, broken parents, grieving widows. Not every village has found favor with your lords over the years. Not all of us can forget what they are."

I meet her gaze with one just as hard. "You think I defend them entirely? I do not. They are imperfect as men and terrible as dragons. I loathed them when I arrived."

"And let me guess...now you love them." There's mockery in her voice. It still stings as she turns away. "You're right. I should not judge. A pretty dress and a warm castle? Not one living husband but three? I cannot blame you for looking past the brutality of the Drakoryans to preserve your own life."

"There are more brutal beings in this world," I say. "Like the ShadowFell. I saw one. I saw what it did to my village. The Drakoryans have never slaughtered humans like that."

She turns back. "No. They did not slaughter. But do not think for a moment that your precious lords do not bring death. Five years ago, my village displeased your Drakoryans. They punished us by burning half the land we farmed. Come the harvest, they still took their due, although it left less for us going into a hard winter." She cocks her head. "You're a girl of the villages. You know most men work hard to provide for their families. I was newly married, to a good man who wanted nothing more than to provide. Because there was less food, he and my father went out one night to hunt. They never came home. A pack of Wolven killed them."

Thera the Healer walks back to the mother, picking up a wooden bowl along the way. She kneels and pulls back the blanket from the woman now sleeping with the baby latched to her breast. Ela has expelled the afterbirth in her sleep. Thera picks it up and puts it in the bowl.

"The Drakoryans laid down fire in our village to protect us from the Wolven," I tell her, but I know I offer a hollow defense and so does she.

"There was no fire to drive away the Wolven that killed my father and husband, Isla. And they would not have gone so far from the village to hunt were it not for the coldness of your dragon men."

I stand silent as she removes the soiled bedding from beneath the woman and places a folded cloth between her legs. Thera the Healer puts the soiled linen aside, covers the woman back up with the blanket, and looks up at me.

"This baby may not survive the winter," she says quietly. "Love who you will, just don't ask me to understand or be grateful for the...protection...of these dragons." She pauses. "Thank you for the herbs." She nods towards the doorway of the tent. "Go, please. I need to boil water to wash linens. Like everything else, clean cloth is in short supply. You'll want to return to your lords."

I feel heat rush to my face as I leave the tent and walk out into the cold. I see Jayx in the distance, talking to Turin. Zyvis is with them, too. I am surprised to see him, but eager to be in their company. Thera's judgement clings to me like a cloak. I decide in that moment that I will return here. I will not hide away in the castle while these people suffer the winter. I can help them, whether I become a lady or not, and I shall.

Twenty-Eight

ZYVIS

I should have stayed at the castle. With my father soon to arrive, he will expect me to be there to greet him. I did not speak to him after leaving the king's castle, but there was a reason for that. I knew he'd ask about the mating, and the Deepening. I did not want to tell him I'd failed at both. I am not ready for his wrath. I'd rather deal with my brothers' disappointment than my father's rage, so I'd headed to the villages to seek out Jayx and Turin. My father will have to wait.

I did not expect to see Isla here. As she approaches, Turin explains that she wanted to deliver herbs to the healer. We've been discussing Thera of Darly, and normally, I would weigh in with some authority, but I feel a defeated man now in every way. Worse still, I am afraid. The ever-present fire in my blood feels weaker. Am I reduced as both man and a dragon, with war on the horizon? These are concerns I keep to myself as I focus on Isla, who seems as surprised to see me as I am to see her.

"Lord Zyvis," she says. "Where have you been? I'd hoped you come to visit me; you've been away since we returned."

There's no judgement in her words, nor in her eyes. There is only kindness that makes me somehow feel worse for letting her down, for letting us all down.

"In these times there is much to attend to." My answer is vague, and she does not press me.

"What did you make of the healer?" Jayx changes the subject, much to my relief.

"I admire her." Isla glances back towards the tent.

"You would admire someone who is so angry?" Turin asks.

Isla fixes my brother with a stern glare. "She has cause for anger and fear, yet puts aside both to do righteous good for her people."

A gust of wind swirls snows around us, threatening to extinguish a fire over which three goats roast on a long spit. They were brought here for men working on the buildings, yet I know these animals will barely feed them. To the left is the village storehouse. It is full with food brought from castle supplies, but with the snows coming early, how long will it last? The sound of an infant's wail floats to us on the wind.

"We should head for home," I say begrudgingly. I am sure my father is there by now. His anger will increase each moment I tarry.

Jayx helps Lyla onto her horse. She smiles down at him. I notice the sword at her side—a real sword. No doubt it is a gift. No doubt it pleased her. I think of how I took her wooden sword the night we were together, how it must have humiliated her. I think this is another reason the Deepening failed. I do not deserve her, and because of my unworthiness, our bloodline will end and my brothers will hate me as my father does.

We surround Isla as we ride, shielding her from the icy

breeze. The fur-lined hood cape shields her face. From time to time I catch a glimpse of her silhouette, the sharpness of her nose, her fair skin. I think of her body, so soft as it yielded to me, her sweet tightness as she turned the tables and unmanned me on the floor of the bedchamber. She is different than I thought she'd be. She is stronger, this woman who clung to life after the ShadowFell slaughtered her village. What a son she would have given me. I feel a catch in my throat as I imagine him. Would he have her red hair? My height?

We ride on. The wind subsides, and the snow is falling sporadically now. Ahead is our mountain, but at the base, near the entrance we use when we go on horseback, is a figure. I tense at the familiar silhouette. My father is walking towards us. I can feel his rage, even from here.

We halt our horses. I dismount from mine as he approaches.

"Zyvis!" His voice booms my name. "What is this? I come for an announced visit to find my son does not greet me? Is this respect?"

"We were seeing to the villagers, Father. We—"

He cuts me off. "We are their rulers. And village needs come second to those of your own kind!" My father's gaze moves past me. "Your brothers should have reminded you of that." His eyes narrow as he spots Isla. "What is your lady doing out of the castle and on horseback?" He searches our faces. "Are you mad? If she were to fall and get hurt, she'd be no use for breeding!"

"Isla is a woman, not a broodmare, Lord Udra." Jayx moves his horse forward. "If this is how you see a mate, if this is how you see Mother, no wonder she cried in the night when we were lads."

My father's expression turns thunderous. This is the first time anyone has mentioned the unspoken tension in the house in which we were raised.

"Such weak lords, letting your woman rule you. You're just like my brothers—always so solicitous of your mother, always coddling." He fixes his angry gaze on Isla. "Remember that you are just a weak village girl with a station only elevated by Drakoryan. Get back inside and count yourself fortunate to view your world from a fine castle."

"Do not speak to her like that!" I step up to my father. I feel no fear. I feel only anger—not for myself, but for Isla.

My father's face turns red. "How dare you..." He raises a gloved hand and I catch it. We are surrounded by heat emanating from both our bodies. Behind us, the horses neigh and dance in fear. They sense what is to happen. In my peripheral vision, I see Turin dismount and rush to pull Isla from her horse as Jayx vaults from his.

I am still holding my father's hand above me as the horses gallop towards the stables. I have stopped his strike.

"Don't you dare insult Isla," I say. "She may be a village girl, but she is far from weak. And had I not wasted so many years being afraid of the likes of you, I'd be worthy of her. I am done being afraid, old man. Go back home."

I push him back. My father is breathing heavily. "You dare speak like that to me!" He erupts into a tower of blue-gray flame. The dragon that appears above me is the one I feared most as a child. It was the one that sparred too roughly when teaching me to fight, the one that dashed me into rocks and chided me for bellowing in pain. Now it looms over me again, seeking to silence and intimidate me. But I am no longer a child. I am a man and a dragon lord, ready to finally stand up and fight for what is mine.

I do not cower. Instead, I erupt into flame and when I come into my own dragon form, I feel him crash into me. I dig my claws into the earth, absorbing the bulk of his body with my own. I will not yield. I will not give. My father steps back. He lifts his head and spreads his wings. His mouth opens wide as he inhales the cold air he would use to ignite the venom in his throat glands and make fire.

I will not allow it. I leap forward, closing my teeth around his neck just below his jowls. The dragon that is my father writhes in my grasp, yet I do not let go. I am in control, both of him and myself. I will not let the anger and loathing he stoked in me guide me any longer. I drag his head down, pressing it to the ground with deliberate strength. My mighty foot pushes into his side as he falls, landing with a sideways thud. My eye darts to his, wild firstwith rage, then fear, before dulling with resignation. I could kill him. He knows this now. I could kill him, but I show strength through mercy.

I will let you go, Father. And when I do, you will beg Isla's forgiveness. If you do not, if you do not treat her and our mother with respect from this day forward, I will come for you. Father or no, I will come for you and make you pay. Do you understand?

His eye blinks slowly. He does. Under my foot, his aging dragon body trembles.

I release him and step back. I will not change until he does. The flame he erupts into is dimmer, smaller. It coalesces quickly into man form. He remains on his side as I transform. As I reach down, offering my hand, my father looks at me. He is breathing heavily. There is blood on his neck, but it is not bad and will heal in the pool. He takes my hand. I fix him with one more hard stare, a warning to remember what he must now do. He meets my eyes briefly and then limps over to where my brothers stand with Isla.

"Forgive me," he says. "I had no cause to offend you. I... just..." He seems to search for his words. He looks confused, as if suddenly wondering why he does what he does. "I will not be staying after all. I should not have come." He turns back to me. "When we next meet again, may I be the father I should have been."

He walks into the distance, and when he is nearly out of sight, my father shifts. He beats his wings slowly as he flies home. As I watch the dark of his form against the sky, I feel a soft pressure on my arm.

"Thank you," Isla says.

I look down at her. "For what? For finally doing what I have been too weak to do my whole life? For defending you only after it was too late?"

"Too late?" She smiles up at me. "It is never too late to give someone a gift. And yours is as useful as any sword or blade."

"I don't understand..."

"My Lord Zyvis," she says. "Today you gave me a lesson—that even the dragon one fears the most can be defeated. Your gift to me is inspiration." I feel her warm hand squeeze mine. "Will you give me one more gift?"

"Anything," I say. There are snowflakes clinging to the lashes of green eyes that warm my soul.

"Come to my room tonight," she says.

Twenty-Nine

ISLA

For all his faults, Lord Zyvis is the most beautiful Lord of Za'vol.

Of course, I would not tell him this. Nor would I tell his brothers. Without the shell of anger, there is a softness about his face that has me truly noticing it for the first time. I lift my hands to touch the soft waves of hair that fall to his shoulders. His lips are sensual under the mustache that meets his short-cropped beard. His eyes are filled with longing, with want. For me.

"I am sorry for the way I treated you."

"Don't," I say, putting my fingers to his mouth. "We start new tonight." I run my hand down the mound of his chest. "Would you disarm me?"

I have left my sword on. I want him to take it off. Tonight, I want him to take the lead. His large hands fall to the strap at my waist. He undoes the buckle and removes the scabbard, wrapping the strap around the handle. He does not place the sword out of my reach. Instead, he carefully lays it on a table by the fire.

When he comes back to me, his hands reach behind me. My gown laces in the back. His eyes are fixed on mine as he unlaces my garment enough to push it from my shoulders. I hold my breath as it falls to a puddle of fabric at my feet. Zyvis has seen me naked, yet I feel as if he now sees me for the first time, too. He cups my breast; my nipple hardens when he grazes it with the pad of his thumb.

His hands are warm as they slide down, molding to the curve of my waist. Zyvis lowers his head. His lips find mine. His kiss is gentle and then commanding as his tongue swoops through my mouth. He lifts me into his muscular arms and moves to the bed. As he lowers me onto the coverlet, I reach for the belt of his leather skirt and unfasten it from the sash that holds it up. It falls to the floor and he is as naked as I am. His huge cock strains towards me. I think of the feel of it in my mouth, the salty taste of him, of his response.

He lowers himself to the bed. His hands are everywhere, the warmth of them blazing a path across my skin. I moan under the heat of his touch. I greet the lust in his eyes without fear. He defeated a dragon for me. He is my champion. I spread my legs in welcome.

Zyvis' eyes flash with gold as he slides his length into me. He begins to move, the surface of his cock undulating as he thrusts. I wrap my legs around him as he sets the rhythm, his fingers twining softly in my hair. Our bodies are fused, his hot, hard one pressed to my pale softness.

"Isla, my flame. You are so sweet. So tight."

I smile. His voice is strained. I am beyond aroused, reveling in the feel of his huge body dwarfing mine. Tonight, he leads the dance. Tonight I will wait for him to bring my pleasure.

When it happens, it is unlike anything I can imagine. He is deep inside me when his cock pulses. It is not a movement, but a wave of energy that seems to come from the center of his hardness, moving out through his shaft into my core, pulsing through the sweet, inner spot and triggering a rush of pleasure so sudden and intense that I scream. I pull him to me with my legs, my body bucking against his. I want to ask him what he did, how he did it, yet I cannot form words. I allow myself to let go, clinging to his strong shoulders as I ride the waves he has created within me.

He is not finished. Not by far. Zyvis drives me to the summit of pleasure twice more, and only when I am hoarse from crying out my bliss do I feel him crown my womb with his hot seed. I pull him to me, looking into his eyes. I want him to see my acceptance, and the love I now feel for him.

When his body stills, I take his hands and press them to my head. "Now." I say. "Please."

I do not have to explain. Zyvis knows what I want. He is ready to finish what we stared in the oracle's chamber in the king's castle. He shows me everything. He shows me his broken childhood, the pain of living in the shadow of a father he could not please, the hundreds of subtle ways Lord Udra pitted him against his brothers, thwarting their chance for the closeness other Drakoryan brothers enjoyed. He shows me his rare happy moments, places he discovered when he flew alone to escape the ever-present feelings of inadequacy. He shows me high mountain falls, herds of snow white deer in fields of red-flowered meadows, the mighty eagles he'd race for fun. He allows me to feel his humiliation at losing the battle for first rights to my body. He lays bare the shame of losing control and nearly killing his own brother, the desolation at having let down his family and his father. Then he shows me the confrontation with his father through his eyes, how his love for me swelled enough to break the chains Lord Udra bound him with. I feel that love now. How deep it runs, now that it is free. Tears course down my face.

I am back inside my own mind but hear his voice in my head. "I love you, Lady Isla of Za'vol."

"And I love you."

We hold each other in the dark. "*All is well*," I whisper to all my mates in my mind. I can feel their happiness. "We are one. We are a family. Our bond is complete.

I think on the words of the oracle Ezador: Two dragons threaten your future, he'd said. One you will help defeat, the other you will defeat alone.

I understand now. The first dragon was Lord Udra. It was my love that helped Zyvis defeat the man who would have kept us apart. I am sure the other dragon is the one that took my sister. I am sure I will one day kill it. I will not believe anyone who tells me differently.

War is coming, and I will fight for the good of my empire, the lost maidens of Branlock, and the other villagers. I will do this as a War Bride, with my beloved Drakoryan mates at my side. The Deepening has been achieved.

I am ready for what comes. But for this moment, I put it all aside, curl up in the safety of Zyvis' protective arms, and sleep.

Preview of "Rebel Bride"

Clang! Clang!

I follow the noise to the village armory, feeling the heat from the open stone structure before I reach it. The wooden frame built around the forge is open with a steeply pitched roof that sheds the snow.

I stand by the outside corner, observing as a Drakoryan lord instructs a villager on the art of hammering red hot metal into a blade. Beside him, another man pushes his newly finished sword into a barrel of water and for a moment, the steam it produces is so thick as to cloud him them from view.

I am here for a reason. I stop, looking for the familiar face. And there he is. While not as tall as Bran, Cyril is still half a head taller than the other village man. But despite his muscular build, he has a somewhat boyish face with ruddy cheeks and a slightly pug nose. Still, many a maiden thinks him handsome. He could have his pick of any of them but has not yet married.

For a moment, I hesitate. Perhaps what I am about to do is wrong. Then I think of Bran, of the bloody shirt, of the awful moments he must have endured as the wolves killed him and my father. I think of my fellow villagers allying themselves with the rulers I blame for the death of my husband. When I am angry enough, I walk into the ironworks. Cyril is carrying an armful of blades to a rack. He has not spotted me yet, and since we are behind the forge, I am out of sight of the Drakoryans. I have learned that the five who stay in the village are lords, and all brothers. Sometimes I catch them watching me, and do not like it.

"Thera!" Cyril finally spots me. He tosses his head, throwing a forelock of hair away from his blue eyes. It's the kind of gesture that charms the other village women. "What brings you here?"

"Curiosity. So much noise. I had to see the cause."

"Swords." He picks one up from beside the rack. Its blade gleams in the cold light. "Any man who agrees to fight will get one."

I cock a brow. "And those who don't pledge allegiance will be as defenseless as we were when we lived across the mountain. Weapons were forbidden then, or have you forgotten?"

Even though it is cold, I lower the hood of my cloak, which is slightly open. I wear a chemise, and over it, a plain dress with a bodice that molds to my breasts. I pretend not to notice how intently Cyril is looking at me. I turn, putting my hand on the hilt of a new blade. "What use are blades against dragons, anyway?"

"They are a weapon of last resort," he says. "The Drakoryans say any dragon that lands will have already been wounded by fire or spear. If they are still alive, we are to attack until the Drakoryans finish them off."

I cross my arms. "Such knowledge and weapons would have been useful when the Drakoryans were burning our land and taking our maidens."

Cyril reaches out and takes my arm. "Mind your tongue, Thera." His voice is low. "Such words bring offense."

I jerk away from him. "Only to cowards who have traded their dignity for a shiny sword and the promise of glory." I soften my tone upon seeing Cyril's wounded expression. "Bran never would have joined this army. He would have only pretended to. Then, when he was armed, he would have avenged our people against these Drakoryan, cutting them down while they were in man form."

"Thera..." He looks around, as if afraid someone will hear. "Bran is no more." He stares into my eyes. "Your period of mourning is long past..."

"Cyril, don't.."

He sighs, exasperated. "Just listen to me, Thera. If you'd only let me ease your loneliness, perhaps you'd not be so angry."

"Only justice will ease my anger," I reply with a shake of my head. "And I'll never take a mate until I find a man strong enough to stand up to the Drakoryan."

Cyril is looking at the swell of my breast. A spasm of want crosses his face. "You'd remain stubborn to your very death? And what of the black dragons? What happens when they come?"

"Black dragons." I utter the words bitterly. "Funny, don't you think, that we've not seen them? And odd that the harvest disappears after we are imprisoned here. The Drakoryans send their lords to live among us. Do you think raising a pint by the fire makes you one of them? This is all a ruse, Cyril. Mark me. They seek to train our men for some future war. None comes here." He's uneasy now, and I take advantage of his uncertainty to press my point. "Don't be their fool, Cyril. If you don't have the backbone to take up arms against the Drakoryan, at the least find the strength to refuse to serve, and to encourage others to refuse as well. Don't be so easily used."

"Cyril of Darly. Have you..." A deep voice from behind interrupts us. I turn and see the speaker is one of the Drakoryans. This one, as always, is in the company of his identical twin. They fall silent, as if surprised to see me.

"Healer, what brings you here?"

"She came to bid me good day." Cyril lays a hand on my shoulder, and given the headway I've made, I can hardly pull away. When his hand closes in a possessive squeeze, however, I do just that.

"I've dallied enough." I pull my hood back over my hair and look up at the two Drakoryans from under its rim. "I apologize if I've taken your loyal subject away from the tasks he performs with such...obedience."

I smile almost sympathetically at Cyril and can tell by the expression in his eyes that I achieved my objective. Through my childhood friend, I have sowed the first seeds of distrust against our Drakoryan masters.

Books in the Drakoryan Brides Series

About the Author

USA Today Bestselling Author Ava Sinclair has been writing sexy romantic fiction for over twenty years, and enjoys creating both believable worlds and relatable characters for her readers.

She lives on a farm in the foothill country of Virginia and enjoys hiking, reading, catering to her cats, and tending to her goats and sheep.

Connect with Ava

Let's be friends. It's possible today thanks to social media. Here's where you can find me.

On Facebook I have a main page, an author's page – both under the name Ava Sinclair - and a private group – Ava's Risque Reading Room.

I'm also on Instagram and TikTok as **authoringava**

Milton Keynes UK
Ingram Content Group UK Ltd.
UKHW020808080823
426520UK00017B/837